RUBY'S RISK

*Westward Home and
Hearts Mail-Order Brides #2*

Marisa Masterson

TABLE OF CONTENTS

ACKNOWLEDGEMENTS

A huge thank you goes to Elaine Manders for inviting me to join this series. In writing this book, I relied on an 1857 map of Missouri based on U. S. surveys. It can be found at https://digital.shsmo.org/digital/collection/Maps/id/95/rec/10.

Thanks also to Christine Sterling Bortner and Amy Petrowich for their help in making my book publication ready. An additional thank you goes to the Ruby's Risk beta readers: Theresa Baer, Becky Bell Bowen, Cindy Edwards, and Lou Klassen.

CHAPTER 1

Eyes followed him as he walked down the street. A burning sensation prickled the back of his neck, helping him feel those eyes on him. The gossip and judgment of the people he'd previously called friends galled him.

Straightening his muscular shoulders, he didn't twitch or look backward to name the people who watched him. After all, it didn't matter since he knew the attitude of the entire town seemed unanimous. They all were sure he had done it.

The entire population of Mills Bluff believed he'd killed his wife.

Elias Kline decided in that moment to move away. How could he raise his son in this atmosphere? Already he'd heard rumbles that questioned whether he should be allowed to keep his child or if Mary's parents should raise him.

Yes, he needed to leave. But where to move to? It would be the same in the other towns nearby. Word of Mary's drowning and Franz's murder had certainly traveled to the surrounding communities.

Leaving wasn't as frightening for him as it might be for other members of the community. After all, he hadn't been born here. No, he'd drifted into Mills Bluff and been accepted as one of them shortly after he returned from the war.

His father had sent him to purchase grain from the mill there. While visiting, he'd stayed the night. The communal support and peace of the people in the town called to his war-weary soul. Too, Mary Schmidt's beauty and apparent interest in him played a big part in his decision to start a smithy here.

As a trained blacksmith, he'd been warmly welcomed, even though he'd been carefully watched at first. Because he'd been raised in a household that spoke only German at home, he was able to attend the Lutheran services done in that language. There he'd met Mary.

The Schmidt family also spoke only German in their home. They were thrilled to have a successful community member who shared a similar heritage take an interest in their only daughter. In fact, they pushed for a quick wedding as soon as his interest became apparent and offered a generous dowry for him to marry their flirtatious daughter.

Mary's forward manner and flirty behavior should have warned him. Later, he cursed himself for not questioning why they'd pushed for him to marry her in such haste. The fact that he'd been the only virgin on their wedding night explained their urgency.

Seven months later, they welcomed a son, a beautifully formed infant who was large for an early baby. Mary had named him Franz, after her grandfather. He called him Frank, arguing that he would need an American name.

While he rarely allowed his mind to consider if Frank was his son, the return of Franz Sauer and his wife to Mills Bluff as well as Mary's recent death brought his repressed doubts to the surface. Five years ago, Sauer and his wife had moved away suddenly, around the same time that he and Mary had wed. He'd heard murmurs about that for weeks. After all, the families of both Sauer and his wife lived in the town. People didn't just pick up and leave their families to move to a nearby town.

That first Sunday in church after Sauer's return, Elias caught the heated glances passing between his wife and the man. After the service, Mrs. Sauer openly snubbed Mary when she approached the woman while dragging Frank behind her. Watching this snub, Elias' large hands had fisted while suspicions formed in his mind.

After church, while Frank napped, he'd fought with his wife about the Sauers. He'd accused her of being pregnant at the time of their wedding. Not answering the accusation, she'd stormed toward the front door, throwing a singsong taunt his way. "Poor Elias, filled with regret at the poor bargain he made!"

Those had been her last words to him. Later that night, the sheriff came to his door with news of

Mary's death. "Odd mark on the back of her neck. Bruised and scraped as if something sat there to hold her in the water." His voice held a thinly veiled indictment of Elias. "Heard you were in a black mood after church today. Franz Sauer have anything to do with that?"

And so, the recriminations and suspicions began. To make things worse, a day after his wife's death, Franz Sauer was found dead with a bullet in the back of his head. Dark accusations about Elias' involvement flew around town. Some folks decided that he'd taken vengeance while other people whispered that Franz had seen him drowning Mary, so Elias killed him.

Now, a month later, people around him showed no signs of forgiving and forgetting. Not that he'd done anything requiring forgiveness. While his in-laws were convinced that jealousy had somehow led to their daughter's death, they were some of the few who didn't place the blame squarely on his shoulders.

Actually, they kept him informed about the talk in town. More than once, his mother-in-law shared with him what Franz Sauer's mother had said about a widower having no business raising a child. She'd hinted that her family had a right to the boy.

No matter what they knew about Frank's parentage, Elias claimed the child as his, had wanted him from the moment that he'd held the blotchy, red bundle. His son was the one constant joy in his life, and he refused to risk losing him. He would not lose him.

He'd go west. Mother Schmidt was right. Frank needed a mother. Elias twisted his mouth wryly. He would need a wife's help as they traveled by wagon as well as when he set up a home and built his business in one of the young western towns.

Marrying one of the local girls was out of the question. He wanted a new start. Besides, he doubted any family in town would look kindly on his offer of marriage with this cloud of mistrust hovering over him.

No, he would write to that agency he'd seen advertised in the paper. Thinking back, he remembered its rather long name—Westward Home and Hearts Matrimonial Agency.

Arriving at his business, he groaned at the lack of customers waiting outside its doors. In the past, men would be lined up with horses to shoe or tools that needed mending. Some even came just to tell a thumper while the day passed by. Until recently, he hadn't had the time to stand around and spin impossible stories like those men.

Now, he'd been tried and convicted in the court of public opinion. He'd been sentenced to isolation, evidently. All the more reason to sell what he could and head to Missouri. Whatever bride that agency sent to him could meet him there.

Keeping the doors to his business shut all day, he lit a lantern and worked in the dim light of his smithy. Coals buried in the ashes of his forge added to the glow as well. He kept his wagon in the back of the long building, near the two horse stalls that stood empty. His own animals were kept at the livery. The stalls were there for horses left by their owners to be shod.

Using the muscles built over long hours at the forge, he pushed the wagon to the middle of the room. Then he pulled a metal trunk from a corner and opened it. During the next hours, Elias carefully packed tools into it before stowing it into the wagon. If only he could pack the carefully built pit that was his forge. He would start over, but at least he would have a future and his son.

Once the tools of his trade were packed onto the wagon, he leaned into it with both hands and pushed the vehicle to the double doors at the back of his shop. He'd retrieve Frank from the boy's grandparents and then pack their clothes.

No, that didn't make sense, he realized. He would pack before getting the boy. Everything needed to be ready when he left town. For some unknown reason, he felt like he needed to sneak away after dark.

Did he truly believe anyone would stop him? The sheriff had no evidence linking him to the two crimes. After all, he was innocent. Would leaving town make him appear guilty? Should he talk with the man to explain why he was leaving?

Since that seemed advisable, he made a stop at the jail before heading to his home. Royce Atkins, the sheriff of Mills Bluff, nodded and harrumphed as he listened. When Elias finished his explanation, the sheriff rose and stretched a hand up to lay it on the much taller man's shoulder. "Don't blame you. I know you didn't do a thing to either your wife or that tomcat Sauer. Folks around town aren't likely to forget their suspicions any time soon, especially since the two victims were born and raised here while you sort of drifted into town."

After shaking hands with Royce, he headed to the door. Crowds had gathered on both sides of the street to stare at the jail. When he opened the door into the cluster of people gathered around it, he called back to the sheriff. "Atkins, you want to head outside before me. Seems there are some folks who want answers."

The sheriff stepped out onto the boardwalk that ran in front of his jail. Then he stepped up onto the bench placed against the front of the building. Holding up his hands, he called for the murmurs of the crowd to cease. "Now, just quiet down and listen. I'm not saying we don't have a murderer in town. I can tell you that I'm doggone certain it's not Elias Kline."

Herman Sauer, Franz's father, stepped forward from the group and shook a fist at Elias. "Don't matter what he says. In my mind, I see you putting a gun to the back of my boy's head. I hear former soldiers kill easily."

Elias opened his mouth to explain that he'd seen enough killing at Gettysburg and Antietam to last a lifetime. He would never willfully shoot another human. His explanation was cut off by Atkins. "No one pinned a badge to your chest, Sauer. I'd best not hear of you taking the law into your own hands. I have a rope to hang any vigilante with, you hear me."

Grumbles and jeers rippled across the crowd. From the women on the other side of the street, Mrs. Sauer began to scream the word "justice" over and over. Her daughter-in-law, the widow, cringed and looked down at her feet while the women around her took up the chant so that the word became like the beat of a drum. Even when the sheriff gestured with his hands and then called for them to quiet down, they refused to stop.

Leaving them to the sheriff, Elias turned his back and headed north to his home. After a month, the level of hatred toward him had grown instead of abating. Today's scene confirmed his decision to head out of town.

His stomach growled, reminding him that he hadn't eaten since breakfast. No time now to stop and eat. Already, most of the day had passed. In another four hours, it would be night, so he needed to hurry with the packing.

The windows of houses he passed seemed to follow him like condemning eyes as if all the way home people stared at him. He had to get out of this town before the persecution drove him crazy.

Finally, at the small home he rented from his in-laws, Elias climbed the two steps and pushed aside the wisteria that had grown too tall. He'd meant to trim it, but too many concerns had filled his time in the month since Mary's death. With his hand on the door, he froze. Sounds were coming from inside his house. Bumps and muted voices drifted out an open window.

Memories of sneaking through the wilderness of Virginia while on patrol came back to him with sudden clarity. The cold fear now was the same as what he'd felt then. Moving back through the wisteria and down the steps, he silently moved to the side of his home and peered in first one window and then the next, hoping to catch a glimpse of the intruders.

At the open window of his bedroom, he spied two shadowy forms. Then a third one, a child joined them. What were his in-laws doing in his bedroom and why were they emptying the drawers of his oak tallboy dresser? It was tempting to speak to them through the window and put a scare into them. Still, he didn't want to draw the neighbors' attention. Even more, he didn't truly want to frighten his in-laws. After all, they'd consistently supported him.

Making his way to the back door not far from his bedroom window, he opened the green door with its black screen and allowed it to slap against the door frame as it closed. That should alert Father and Mother Schmidt that he was there.

The pine boards squeaked as he made his way across the kitchen. His mother-in-law had been busy. The fragrant smell of fresh bread, along with the aroma of stew, tempted him, and he moved through the room towards the hallway. He stopped at the first door on the left and leaned against the frame. "What's going on?"

While he'd been sure he had made noise, both of the Schmidts jumped at his question. Frank squealed with delight and ran to his father. He hoisted the four-year-old into his arms and hugged him, carefully not to squeeze too hard. Small arms looped around his neck and clutched him tightly.

"Daddy, Grandma says you and I are takin' a trip. Did you know that?" His son pulled back so he could watch Elias' face as he spoke, confusion clear in both his voice and his expression.

Elias turned to his in-laws with an eyebrow quirked. "I'd planned a trip, but I didn't think they knew about it. Did someone see me packing the wagon at the smithy today?"

Helga Schmidt shook her head at his question, gray ringlets bobbing as she did so. "No, no one.

I've heard something and knew you must leave quickly. Tonight." Her voice shook as she spoke. Her husband stood in the shadow of the darkened bedroom, saying nothing. She gestured with a hand for him to stand next to her. When he joined her near the dresser, Elias read the grim distress on his face.

"What do you say, Father Schmidt? Are things as dire as Mother Schmidt says?" Elias hoped for further details. His father-in-law was better at concisely explaining a situation than his wife.

The man cleared his throat. "Probably much worse. Sauer is planning to hang you tonight and snatch the boy. He's lost a son and knows that Frank is his only living link to Franz."

Elias' face flattened as though he'd taken a punch. No one had ever voiced the truth before this. A small part of him had hoped that Frank had been born early and was his.

No, this boy was his. An illicit act didn't make Franz Sauer a father. The day in and day out nurturing bonded father and son. Frank was and always would be his son.

Mary's father was apologizing, forcing Elias to discipline his thoughts and emotions. "—all for the best. We left it up to her to tell you, though we knew the truth. You've been all we could hope for in a son-in-law. The boy loves you and we don't want him to lose another parent."

Nodding his head, Elias stood silent for a moment. Then he asked, "Did you have a plan?"

Josef Schmidt gave a grim, tightlipped smile. "Of course. Don't I always?"

The man outlined a plan to send Elias off with the Schmidts' team and wagon. Since his own was already partially packed, Elias interrupted him. "I'll take my own wagon, but having you get your team from the livery will create less suspicion. After all, Mac at the livery is good friends with Sauer. We'll drive your wagon to the smith after dark and hook the team to my vehicle. You can take my team later to reclaim your wagon."

Father Schmidt put an arm around his wife's shoulders and shook his balding head. "No, we're going with you. We don't want to lose our grandchild."

Elias kissed his son's brown curls and then set him back on his own feet. "You'll be safe if you stay here. That way, you can sell things for us—the smithy, this house, and your own. We'll need funds to set up somewhere."

A look passed between the couple. Without a word, his father-in-law turned back to Elias and nodded his agreement. In the next hour, Elias signed the deed to the smithy over to Josef. Then he ate a meal as Helga packed a hamper with sandwiches, fruit, and cookies. She'd already packed Frank's clothes and toys. Josef finished packing Elias' things while the others were in the kitchen.

At dusk, Josef headed to the livery and asked Mac's helper for the wagon and his team. Once back, he drove the wagon up the alley behind the house. Elias hauled the trunks easily and loaded them into the wagon. The hamper and a stack of quilts came next, carried by Helga and Josef.

Frank stood just inside the screen door and clutched his stuffed rabbit, his thumb in his mouth. Since his mother's death, the little boy had resumed sucking that thumb. They'd broken him of the habit just after the new year, but Elias hated to get after him now about it. Frank needed whatever comfort he could find after the month they'd just experienced.

Inky darkness hid the wagon's movement. No one stopped them as Josef drove it to the back door of the smithy. Opening the padlock, Elias handed it and the key to Josef. "It's yours now. Thank you for taking care of this for us."

With the double doors opened, the team pulled the wagon inside the dark smithy. Since he'd allowed them to die out that day, no coals glowed in the forge. Their absence caused a shiver of fear to go down Elias' spine. This was the end. Would he escape the plans the Sauers had for him? Something about the cold, gray ash in the forge seemed to hint at bad things to come.

Telling himself to stop being a superstitious German, he helped unhitch the team and led it to the other wagon. As Josef hitched it up again, Elias transferred the trunks, blankets, and food to his wagon. He stretched and tied down a tarp over the load, leaving a spot open for Frank to crawl through. He wanted his son to be able to sleep under the tarp like a tent or even to be able to get under it in case of rain.

Embracing Mary's parents, he promised, "We will meet again. I promise to write so you know where we are, but I won't use my name. Look for letters from Joe Smith."

With a final kiss for their grandson, the Schmidts stepped back from the wagon and watched Elias guide the team out of the building. They waved a silent goodbye. As he'd been told by the adults, Frank stayed quiet through the process. Without making a sound, Frank pulled his thumb from his mouth and returned their wave. Then he leaned into his father for comfort.

It had worked! With a whisper dropped into an ear here and there, she'd managed to stir up many of the people on Main Street. Having them form a wall that Elias Kline walked into when he left the jail had been a stroke of good luck. More than she could have hoped for, really, considering how slow to act and stupid men could be.

The man had no right to the child. The boy was even named Franz. It was a message that the mother wanted him to be raised as a Sauer.

She would begin her rumors again. Tonight. She would have him by tonight. The women were sympathetic to her, after her terrible loss. They would push their men into action.

Vigilante justice! Not justice. Only she knew that. Elias Kline's lynching would simply be a means to finally get what was rightfully due her.

CHAPTER 2

"Well, that's the end of home and family."

Ruby muttered those words as she watched her sister and her groom leave the church. She stood back, away from the church steps and out of the small crowd of well-wishers. As Emmie and Thomas exited, rice showered them. Emmie giggled and tried to keep up as her husband wrapped an arm around her and ducked the shower thrown their way by friends and family.

She was happy for her sister. Ruby mentally chastised herself for the glum words she'd said out loud. After all, Emmie should marry and have a family. She was glad her baby sister hadn't turned into a spinster like herself. There just hadn't been time to marry.

Too many things and people had kept Ruby Hastings busy over the years. Her widowed father and her siblings had needed her to make a home for them. After Papa's death five years earlier, just Onie and Emmie had needed her. Then that business last year had sent Onie running from town in the night so only Emmie remained at home with Ruby. She hadn't heard a word from him or about him since then. Of course, she couldn't expect to. Not with that bounty on his head.

Now, Emmie had married, and Ruby would be alone. Years of quiet stretched dauntingly out in front of her.

True, she had various interests that would help fill her days. Already, she volunteered weekly at the local orphans' home where she taught the girls things such as sewing, knitting, and rug braiding. As an additional source of income, she gave weekly piano and voice lessons to many local children. She adored anything that brought her into contact with children.

Emmie and Thomas were in the buggy now. Friends had decorated it with a long daisy chain.

The length amazed Ruby and she wondered where they'd found enough flowers to make it. Wherever they had, the chain and its blossoms transformed the buggy into something magical and Ruby couldn't help sighing. Even though she gave the appearance of being an active and settled old maid, weddings made her long for a magical and romantic happening.

Nothing magical ever happened at the quilting bees or church socials that made up her life. Those were better described as plodding and mundane. Still, she had friends and a routine. Best remind herself to be happy with it.

She needed to shake off this morose attitude before arriving at the wedding luncheon. This was her girl's day, the closest Ruby expected to come to marrying off a daughter. She needed to enjoy it.

Emmie had been like a daughter. Emerald, really, though neither of them liked that name. Onie's name was worse, though. Who would name a boy Onyx? A jeweler by trade, Papa had insisted each child be given the name of a precious stone. Mama, an accommodating woman, hadn't tried to change his mind. Ruby's name wasn't so bad, she supposed, but Emmie hated hers. After all, Papa once told her he chose it because a ruby was red just like a paper heart at Valentine's Day and she'd had his heart since her birth. Still, the sisters joked that their names would be better fitted to saloon girls rather than good, Christian women.

Before leaving the church to head to Cousin Lavinia Sprague's large house for the luncheon, Ruby headed around the church. She had a strong urge to visit her parents' graves. First, she went into the church. Picking up the vase of bridal wreath and roses, she took it off the altar and carried it outside. There, she laid it next to Mother's headstone. If life had been fair, Mother should have been there to enjoy the flowers.

Mother hadn't been strong, she remembered after Onie's birth. Even five-year-old Ruby had realized that. Her brother had been everyone's pride and joy. She had been delighted by the baby and couldn't recall ever being jealous of him. She'd been sure he would be her only sibling. Emmie's birth seven years after came as a surprise.

Looking down at the grave, memories and feelings from nearly twenty years prior flooded Ruby. She still didn't understand why her parents had wanted another baby. The pregnancy had been dangerous for her mother. As a twelve-year-old, she had been very aware of that as she'd listened to the adults discuss it. Certainly, her parents could have chosen not to have another baby. Everyone had a choice in whether or not they had babies, didn't they?

At the orphanage, Ruby saw little ones who'd been abandoned with notes indicating their mothers couldn't or didn't want to provide for the babies. Maybe this proved that babies came whether a woman wanted them or not?

Regardless of whether her parents planned to have Emmie, she'd been born, and Mother had died. Today, Thomas made nineteen-year-old Emmie his wife and Ruby became obsolete.

Soon after the luncheon, the newlyweds planned to travel by train to his Boston home. There, his family would welcome Emmie with open arms. She would no longer need the spinster sister who had raised her.

For goodness sakes, she had to snap out of this maudlin stream of thought. Allowing herself one last sigh, she turned from the grave and almost tripped over a woman who approached from behind.

Reaching out to steady the older woman, Ruby immediately apologized. "I am very sorry, madam. My mind had wandered so I didn't realize you were behind me."

"My dear, it's no problem." The small woman laid a comforting hand on Ruby's forearm. "I do love reading the headstones and trying to decide what each stone reveals about the people buried beneath them."

Ruby thought that seemed odd but refrained from commenting. She hated the death represented by these stones and only visited out of respect. Nevertheless, she smiled in response to the woman's words, encouraging her silently to continue speaking.

The woman accepted the smile as the invitation it was. "I noticed earlier how sad you seemed. Because of your parents, no doubt." Looking first at the graves and then back to the younger woman, she continued without waiting for an answer. "Well, it's certainly reasonable to miss them on such a special day with their youngest daughter marrying."

Now, the woman did pause as she searched for a response in Ruby's expression. When the younger woman only nodded and gave the strange woman a tight-lipped smile, she prodded Ruby further.

"Come, my dear. I watched you at the wedding. You tried to conceal it, but your distress still showed."

At those words, Ruby blanched. She didn't know her feelings were so transparent. Stuttering with embarrassment, she frantically searched her mind for a change of topic. Since the woman was unknown to her, she pursued that. "You must be one of Thomas's relatives if you're visiting for the wedding."

Graciously, the woman allowed her to change the direction of their conversation to this topic.

"My, yes! Thomas's mother is my favorite cousin. Why, we were raised like sisters." She smiled wistfully as she spoke, remembering her girlhood. "In fact, I'm even Thomas's godmother. Not having been blessed with children of my own, I've poured as much time and love into Thomas as my life with Mr. Crenshaw allowed."

The mention of her husband threw another conversational lifeline Ruby's way. "Oh, is your husband waiting for you at the luncheon?"

A shadow of grief passed over the woman's otherwise serene face. "Sadly, no. He's buried in Boston. What a man the Congressman was! He had big dreams for settling the West, my dear, and fought to allow for the expansion of our great nation."

Not sure what to say, Ruby mumbled a polite expression of sympathy over the woman's loss. She ignored the comment about the westward expansion. After all, her life was in Massachusetts and she'd barely paid attention to politics.

At her sympathetic murmur, the woman waved her hand dismissively and took up her earlier conversation. "I was remiss. Allow me to make myself known to you, Miss Hastings. I'm Millie Crenshaw of Boston."

Nodding her head to Mrs. Crenshaw, Ruby fidgeted nervously. She needed to make her way to the luncheon and wondered how to steer the woman in that direction. Deciding a direct approach would work best with this forthright woman, she voiced her suggestion. "I believe we'd best make our way to the luncheon or we'll miss seeing them cut the cake. Please, will you walk with me?"

As they made their way around the side of the brick church and headed south to her cousin's home, Mrs. Crenshaw resumed her gentle interrogation. "But, tell me, why do you seem so sad? I sense that it isn't about your parent's absence. I sincerely want to know, and I am a very good listener."

As a typically private person, Ruby couldn't explain what led her to confide in this stranger. No matter how many times she told the story through the years, she always wondered about that. Perhaps the emotions of the day had weakened her usual reserve. For whatever reason, she poured out her feeling of uselessness because of Emmie's leaving and wallowed in self-pity as they walked.

When they reached Cousin Lavinia's home, she stopped them and met Millie Crenshaw's eyes. "Thank you for listening. I feel much better. Ready now, in fact, to meet the others again and appreciate you letting me ramble."

Reaching out, Mrs. Crenshaw took her hand and squeezed it before dropping it again. "It was not rambling. You need a solution for your sense of being useless and adrift. It so happens that I have one."

Her confident insistence led Ruby to look more closely at the woman. Millie's eyes gleamed with secret knowledge, and a sort of coaxing expression lit her face.

"You, Miss Hastings, need to get married."

Ruby laughed ruefully in response to that. "Mrs. Crenshaw, you make it sound so easy. I'm a thirty-two-year-old spinster."

"Tish tosh! It is easy." She patted Ruby's arm. "At least for me. But let's not wait out here. If you want, we will speak further after the luncheon. I plan to spend the night at the hotel."

The house, when they stepped into it, resounded with laughter and cheers. As the women entered the room, Emmie clapped her hands with delight. "Finally, both of them are here." She smiled at her sister before continuing, "After all, I couldn't cut my cake without the dearest person to me watching." Then she laughed. "Of course, that was before I married Thomas."

Laughing with her sister, Ruby moved to stand near the table. All the while, her heart bled. Emmie had summed it up nicely. Without saying it directly, she had confirmed that Ruby had been replaced and removed from her spot of honor in Emmie's life and heart. Oh, she knew her sister would always love her. The love they would share in the future would be different, though, and Emmie would be different as she matured into her role of wife and, God willing, mother.

Emmie held the knife to the cake and Thomas placed his hands over hers while he whispered a private message into her ear. A giggle and a deep chuckle melded into one sound as the two cut the marzipan-covered fruit cake. After giving each other a small taste of it, Lavinia took over cutting pieces to serve the guests.

Mrs. Crenshaw spoke quietly at her side. "They make a beautiful picture, standing in front of the large dining room window and the sun surrounding them. With that light blue dress and her lovely long, blonde curls, your sister is like a doll come to life." Then she lowered her voice. "My dear, I am surprised this wasn't held at your home."

Shaking her head, Ruby indicating how impossible that would have been. "Even though Father was a watchmaker and jeweler, we didn't live in a large house. Ours has only a small dining room." With a discreet gesture in Lavinia's direction, she confided, "Besides, my cousin loves to show off her home and is the consummate hostess. How could I deny her the opportunity to give them this gift?"

"If your cousin is a born hostess, what are you?" The woman asked those words kindly. Still, Ruby felt like an interview had started.

"Me? Well, I suppose you'd say I am a born nurturer." She'd certainly taken easily to her role of mother when Emmie had been born.

"Hmm. Exactly what I thought. Yes, I can help you, Miss Hastings."

The couple drove off soon after, showered with a chorus of well-wishes and cheers. Cousin Lavinia stood on the top step of her front porch and lifted her arms to indicate she wanted attention. Addressing the group on her front lawn, she invited, "Come inside to pick up a wrapped piece of cake to take home with you. Remember, for all of our maiden ladies, place it under your pillow tonight and dream of the man you'll marry."

It was a silly superstition and many in the crowd guffawed or chuckled. For the first time in years, she dared hope that mousy and plain Ruby Hastings might marry. She wouldn't put the slice of cake under her pillow, but she did plan to speak with

Millie Crenshaw and discover how that woman planned to help her.

Elias Kline had escaped!

She'd followed the men that night. With a dark hood over her hair and the cloak wrapped around her black dress, she knew she was invisible. Hidden like that, she still held back in the shadows to listen and watch.

The Schmidts! Such stupid people. They helped him. The men said as much after they went to the livery stable. Kline's horses were there while Schmidt's were gone.

Tonight, she would whisper about searching for them. The boy was hers, all she had left.

CHAPTER 3

"So, I decided that men in the West needed wives if the territories were to be settled and civilized. You can play a role in that." Mrs. Crenshaw picked up her china cup after she finished speaking and took a delicate sip of tea.

Alone in the hotel suite with the woman, Ruby allowed herself to sink back against the chair. She'd been taught to never allow her spine to touch the back of a seat. This time, however, she gave in and did so as the woman's explanation rolled over her. Be a mail-order bride. Go west and leave everyone she knew. The idea overwhelmed her, at first.

Then she realized the potential. She could begin her life again with a man who also wanted to start a new life. Ruby could shed the label of "old maid" like a snake shed its skin.

No, maybe thinking about snakes wasn't good. That comparison suddenly made the whole venture seem evil somehow. She wouldn't allow herself to dismiss Mrs. Crenshaw's offer so quickly.

Peering at the woman over her own cup, Ruby voiced the question burning in her mind. "How long would I need to wait for the right match?" Now that the possibility existed, Ruby decided to leap before she could lose her nerve.

A satisfied smile creased Mrs. Crenshaw's composed countenance. Rising, she slipped into the bedroom and quickly returned holding a letter.

The woman looked down at the letter in her hand and sighed. "This one troubled me, so I've carried it in my reticule since I received it a week ago. I've been praying over it, asking the Lord to direct me to the wife for this man."

"Is there something wrong with him that his match required divine intervention?"

Mrs. Crenshaw's steady blue eyes met hers and she smiled graciously. "No, I think any woman would be blessed to have him. He's a believer, though Lutheran which might bother your Methodist sensibilities. He's a hard worker, doesn't drink, and is a good family man."

Ruby gave a short, disbelieving snort. Indelicate for a lady to do, she knew, but the moment seemed to call for it. "Now I know what's wrong with him. He's too good to be true." Searching Millie's honest gaze, she asked, "Do you have any doubts about what he's written in his letter?"

"None at all. No, the problem lies with his wife."

At those words, Ruby choked on the sip of tea she'd just taken, and a few drops landed on her amethyst gown. "Wife? You think my perfect match is a bigamist!" Her cup and saucer clattered as she placed them back on the table and rose.

Millie Crenshaw also rose. With a straight spine and the look of a general directing a battle, she motioned for the other woman to sit once again.

Reluctantly, Ruby lowered herself into the chair. Shock marred her previously hope-filled face, but she decided to allow the woman a chance to explain.

Apologizing, Mrs. Crenshaw also resumed sitting. "I've made a mess of this. I am so sorry. Perhaps it would be best if you read the letter yourself." She held it across the table and, with great curiosity and more than a little dread, the younger woman took it.

The paper was plain, the type you'd buy in the store a sheet at a time. The handwriting seemed heavy on the paper, the letters thick and pushed into the surface. Was he impassioned as he wrote or merely a very strong man?

Dear Westward Home and Hearts Matrimonial Agency,

I head west soon. As a widower, I need a wife to make my trip west comfortable and possible. For this reason, I am writing to you.

A month ago, my wife Mary drowned. She left me with a young son to raise. Mary wasn't willing to be much of a wife and mother, but the boy misses her fiercely.

I can provide for a wife. I'm a blacksmith and had a good business until this ugly problem with Mary's death. To tell the truth, some in Mills Bluff, where I lived for five years, want to call me a murderer. I've been a son, a soldier, a husband, a father, a business owner, but never have I been a murderer.

I attend the Lutheran church in town and am at service each week. Maybe a prospective wife might like to know that I don't drink, gamble, associate with easy women, and am not given to violence.

Let me make it plain that I trust you to find the right woman for me. I didn't do a good job of choosing my first one. My need is great. I ask for a woman who is motherly, skilled in the areas of cooking, sewing, and housewifery and is not a shrew.

One last thing I beg you to consider for me. Please, send a wife who has never married and has kept herself from the company of men. This proved to be a great problem in my marriage. For myself, I've always practiced purity and fidelity and would like that in my bride.

For my son's sake, I ask that the woman want to be a good mother. She should be a person who would happily sing to a little boy at bedtime or read to him from his Mother Goose book.

Am I asking for too much? When I read over the letter and fear that I am. What woman would take on an uncertain life with a man who's assumed a new name? I'm praying, and perhaps you will as well, that such a woman is out there and wants to make her home with a discouraged widower and his sad son.

I wait in Stewartville, Missouri, for your response. I plan to follow the old Oregon Trail and venture westward until I find a newly established town needing a blacksmith. I expect there will be one somewhere in Nebraska.

Please telegraph me if you find my perfect bride. I will wire additional funds for a train ticket. She will be able to go by train to St. Joseph, where I will meet her. We will marry and head out soon after

In faith, I am sending both the fee and additional monies for telegrams. I pray I will hear *from you. I must leave no later than August so know that plans will change if a match hasn't happened before then.*

Respectfully yours,

Ezra King

(formerly Elias Kline of Mills Bluff, Indiana)

Reading the letter through once more, Ruby lifted her head and stared at nothing in particular. Mrs. Crenshaw softly cleared her throat to gain her attention.

"Do you understand now what I meant about his wife? He's been ill-used in his marriage and, I believe, falsely accused. Add to that, you will be marrying a stranger." The woman's tone held a matter-of-fact quality and she was careful, Ruby noted, to keep any persuasion out of her voice.

"I've been told that a woman doesn't know her husband until after living with him as his wife." Those words acted as Ruby's consent, and Mrs. Crenshaw knew it. The older woman's expression relaxed as she explained what needed to be done before Ruby boarded the train.

"Sister, this is so unlike you. What can you be thinking?"

Emmie stridently shrieked those words as she came through the back door. Ruby was surprised that the newlyweds had already returned from their wedding trip. She hadn't expected Emmie to read the letter until Ruby had been safely gone from their hometown and on the way to her new life.

No matter how many prayers she whispered, obstacles still blocked her marriage to Elias. First, Cousin Lavinia tried to talk her out of marrying, saying she needed to be content with the unmarried lifestyle she'd been called to. "After all, St. Paul said it was better to be single."

During that conversation Ruby had listened dutifully to her older, more sophisticated cousin, allowing the woman to say what she wanted. After the woman had wound down like a clockwork toy, she spoke calmly and confidently. "Thank you, Lavinia. I needed to be reminded that remaining single is a calling. I know now that I don't have any such calling and believe with all of my being that the Lord is opening this opportunity for me to bless a widower and his son."

Lavinia had sputtered and made ominous predictions. Nothing she said changed Ruby's mind, so the woman agreed to help her pack up the contents of the house.

The next obstacle involved Elias. After Mrs. Crenshaw telegraphed him, she sent a telegram to Ruby, letting her know to expect funds for her ticket. Two days passed and yet no money arrived. She could have paid for the ticket, easily having enough money to do that. The principle of the thing kept her from doing it. After all, he needed to prove that he wanted her to come. It was an act of faith and acceptance to send her that money.

Finally, on the third day, a boy arrived with the message about the funds. After collecting them from the Western Union office, Ruby went directly to the train depot. The ticket tucked away in her reticule affirmed the reality of the decision she'd made for her future.

The unexpected visit from Emmie was a blessing, not an obstacle. Even though her sister was upset, she nevertheless looked radiantly happy.

Ignoring her younger sister's opening comment, Ruby rose and embraced her. "I can see that marriage agrees with you. At least so far."

Emmie snorted. "Yes, I love being married, but I knew Thomas before I married him."

"Does any wife truly know her husband before they live together?" The words were said calmly, with the barest hint of question.

The younger woman froze and looked to her sister. "Are you hinting at something to do with my husband?"

Aghast, Ruby quickly denied that. Putting a hand to her sister's cheek, she smiled down into the girl's face. "Of course not. We're talking about how I am approaching marriage. This has nothing to do with my new brother-in-law. He's wonderful, as far as I can tell."

Used to being cossetted, Emmie soaked in the reassurance her sister gave her. Then she resumed questioning Ruby's decision.

"How can you go west and leave me? I won't have any family left, other than Lavinia." Emmie might be a married woman, but she was also a nineteen-year-old. Her immaturity showed in the self-absorption she betrayed.

"You have Thomas and his family. They seem to already love you. I was especially impressed by how sweet your mother-in-law is to you." Firm but gentle, Ruby reminded Emmie that she'd chosen to marry and move away.

Her sister's frown melted away. "Yes, she's even planned a party to introduce me to their friends." Emmie went on with the details of the proposed event, forgetting for the moment about her sister's marriage.

Deciding she would ignore Emmie's qualms, Ruby chose to distract her by suggesting they fill a trunk. "What would you like to have in your own home? Let's pack a trunk for you. It can travel back by train with you today." The older sister had already picked through the kitchen items she couldn't bear to leave behind. She was happy to offer what was left to her sister.

Of course, Emmie had been showered with gifts by friends. Still, she easily managed to fill a small trunk with items. As she chose them, the sisters shared memories associated with mundane items that had played a role in their everyday life. It was a wonder what a platter or a doily could trigger in their memories and made for a sweet day spent together.

After a brief discussion about the house, during which Emmie tried once again to talk her out of leaving, the women determined not to sell it. "Lavinia will watch over it. You and she can decide on any repairs that might be needed in the future. Perhaps you might want to stay in the home during summers to get out of that hot city."

Throughout the day, Ruby steered the conversation back to Emmie and her life. She'd always tried to put her sister first. In fact, she did that with many people since she wanted the folks in her life to feel cared for by her.

Brushing dust from her brown skirt, she rolled down the cuffs of her brown-striped shirtwaist. "Well, that's done. It never hurts to have a few things from home around you to remember your life here."

"Thank you, Sister, but I couldn't forget the wonderful childhood you gave me." Emmie hugged her and, kissing her cheek, pinned her broad hat back in place.

They'd paid the boy next door a nickel. He ran to the depot and asked for someone to come by before the train to Boston. A knock on the door an hour later, a man arrived for the trunk.

While neither had cried when Emmie left after her wedding, both sisters dabbed at teary eyes since this parting would be more permanent. A kind, stoop-shouldered man helped Emmie onto the seat of the wagon where she carefully spread the skirts of her smoky-lavender traveling suit. Then, as he set the team into motion, the younger sister called back, "I love you, Ruby!"

The cloud of dust stirred up by the wagon swallowed her words. No matter, Ruby had them held close to her heart. She'd raised a kind woman, and she was proud of that.

Her own trunks stood near the front door, in the small entryway. As she walked past them, her eyes focused on the mirrored hall tree. How she wished she could take a few pieces of furniture with her. Really, why couldn't she?

True, they would be traveling by wagon. Any trunks and household goods could follow by train. She'd simply send them forward to a train station. Her things could wait for her arrival. If they didn't settle in that town, she'd send the items onward by rail again until they found a place to establish their home.

Determined to ask the boy next door to run to the train station again, she opened the front door. A young woman stood outside it with her hand raised to knock. The two exchanged a surprised gasp.

Quickly composing herself, Ruby smiled a welcome to the red-haired girl who looked to be about Emmie's age. "Hello. Can I help you?"

Before the girl could speak, a mewling cry sounded from the basket at her feet. Ruby wondered if the girl was trying to find a home for a cat. If so, she would have to send her away.

The girl glanced down at the basket. Picking it up, she held the wicker container out to Ruby. When she only stared at it dumbly, the girl shoved the basket into Ruby's arms.

"He told me you'd take her. With Alicia dying and all, don't seem like no one else can see to the wee thing." The mention of Alicia pricked Ruby's memory of the night Onie and the girl decided to run away together. She'd scraped together as much money for them as she could. In addition, she sent along pieces of jewelry that held little sentimental value. It was that jewelry that brought a bounty down on Onie's head.

In the next town over, her brother stopped to sell a brooch. Hot on the couple's heels, Hiram Brogan found out about the sale and claimed that Onie had stolen the piece from him. By that time, the young lovers had boarded a train for Chicago and Alicia's angry father decided to cause whatever trouble he could for the man who took his daughter.

After Ruby became involved, the sheriff of both her town and that one believed that Hiram had lied about owning the brooch. Still, the vengeful man put a price on Onie's head. With the help of a Boston detective, he circulated wanted posters indicating that Onyx Hastings was wanted on charges of kidnapping. As a wealthy man, he offered a one-thousand-dollar reward. Though the sheriff protested that he wouldn't arrest Onie if the man was returned to him, Hiram insisted that he had a right to put out whatever poster he wanted.

So far, Onie had evaded the man's attempts to reclaim his daughter. Ruby didn't believe Hiram had any leads to his daughter's whereabouts. If it was true that Alicia had died, would that change Hiram's search?

A wail slipped past the blanket covering the basket and penetrated Ruby's heart. She pulled back the piece of gray wool and looked into a red and puckered face. The infant was old enough to focus on her face once she realized she was no longer covered. With an intense interest in the person who stared at her, the little girl ceased her noise and smiled with her little pink posy mouth. Ruby was enchanted by the grin on a face that resembled her brother.

"How old is she?" Ruby tore her gaze away from the cherub and looked at the red-haired messenger.

The girl shrugged. "Not sure to the day. Expect it's all in that letter he put in the basket."

Fishing around the edges of the basket, under the infant's bedding, Ruby retrieved a damp envelope. It was just like her brother to fail to plan for the baby wetting both her bedding and the letter.

"Are you a friend of Onie's?" She wondered how this girl happened to be the one entrusted with the baby.

"Sort of. He and Alicia rented a cabin on Pa's farm. Onie helps Pa and Pa gives him a place to live and lets them eat meals with us. Alicia helped ma before she passed." The girl's mouth twitched and Ruby could see she worked to hold back tears. She guessed that her sister-in-law had become a good friend to this girl.

Suddenly realizing that she was carrying on this conversation in full view of the neighbors, Ruby hurried the girl into the house. Directing her to go into the parlor, she followed behind and set the basket in the middle of the claw-foot parlor table.

The girl, Anna, as she'd introduced herself as she entered the home, protested when Ruby told her to sit down. "Oh no, ma'am. I mustn't. I have to get back on the train for home. Onie said you'd give me money for the fare." She looked hopeful as she said those last words and the older woman nodded.

The baby let everyone know she'd been ignored long enough. With a cry, she began to shake the basket with her movements. Afraid that the infant would roll out of the basket and onto the floor, Ruby raced to the parlor table while Anna looked on stupidly. Obviously, it was only by God's mercy that the child had arrived safely.

"Miss Ruby, I have to get back!" Anna wailed the words, dismissing any concern for the baby.

Ruby cradled her niece for the first time, determined that Anna could wait a minute or two. The baby's crystal-blue eyes were the same as Alicia's. Otherwise, her sandy brown hair, dimpled chin, mouth, and nose resembled Onie and Emmie. She brought to Ruby's mind memories of Emmie as a baby.

Ignoring the baby's wet diaper, she cuddled the little one close. The baby settled against the crook of Ruby's arm and gripped the fabric of her shirtwaist. It was a marvel that the child showed no fear at being held by a stranger. It was as if she sought someone to love and care for her. Someone to mother her.

"How can I write to Onie? Where do I send a letter?" She wasn't going to let Anna get away without finding out the details.

The girl shook her head. "He's planning to move on, he said. I expect I'll see him tonight, though, if you want me to tell him a message."

Moving out of the parlor, Ruby took her reticule down from its spot on the hall tree. Opening it one-handed proved to be tricky. Nonetheless, she managed it and removed money for the girl from her coin purse. "This should get you a ticket. Please, if there's extra, give it to my brother to help him."

Almost sullenly, the girl gave a nod. She reached to take the money from Ruby who held onto it firmly. "Tell my brother I am leaving home to marry. I'll travel to St. Joseph, Missouri, to meet my husband. From there, we're following the Oregon Trail." Directing a no-nonsense look at the girl, she ordered, "Now repeat it back to me."

Anna retold the message three times before Ruby was satisfied and allowed her to take the money. Once she had it in hand, the girl threw a hurried goodbye in her direction and rushed from the house. She followed with the baby in her arms and watched from the doorway as Anna ran down the street like a person running from a pack of wolves.

Turning to go back inside, Ruby noticed a carpetbag placed near the front door. Lifting it, she carried it to the kitchen and rested it on the table. She set the baby next to it. "Let's hope, little one, that this bag contains diapers because you need to be bathed and changed."

The small attic housed some of Emmie's baby things still. It amazed Ruby that she hadn't offered anything in it to Emmie that day. Now she was glad that the clothes, toys, and glass bottles she'd packed away years before were available for her use. She'd need rubber nipples, though. One bottle had been tucked into the basket, but it wouldn't be enough.

Making a bed for the baby on the parlor sofa, Ruby pulled chairs up against it so the little one wouldn't roll off and placed the bathed infant into the makeshift crib. The little girl immediately grabbed for her feet and tried to put one into her mouth. Laughing at that, Ruby watched the girl for a moment before opening the letter from Onie.

Dear Sis,

I'm sending you my dearest possession. My daughter, Letty Louise Hastings, was born April 30. Alicia adored her and said the hardships we suffer were worth it so we could be together and have this angel child. Unfortunately, my wife took a fever within a week of the baby's birth.

I've tried with the help of the McNearys to care for the baby. I can't do it, I've discovered. Two days ago, a bounty hunter came nosing around. It's time for me to move on.

Please keep her for me. You are her best chance for a loving home.

Your loving brother,

Onyx Hastings

Poor Onie! He'd thrown away his teaching position, all for the love of a woman who had died. Calculating, she reasoned that the baby was two-months-old. It was a wonder that he hadn't sent Letty to her earlier. If he had, she wouldn't have committed herself to a mail-order marriage.

She'd made a commitment and would honor it. Letty would go with her to St. Joseph. Her groom wanted an unmarried woman who had lived a pure life. Well, she fit that description. Now, she came with a baby. He would simply have to understand the circumstances and accept Letty.

It never occurred to her to leave the baby at an orphanage or give her over to her mother's family.

Hiram Grogan was a man who always appeared red-faced with anger. She didn't even consider telling him about the baby.

She did, however, send two letters. One went to Emmie to tell her about the baby. In the other, she sent a cry for help to Emmie's father-in-law, giving him a detailed retelling of Onie's situation. The man kindly offered to look into it when they spoke the day before the wedding. In her note to him, she suggested that a poster declaring Onyx Hastings innocent of all charges be sent out. As a lawyer, she trusted him to find a solution to Onie's problem, and Onie wasn't guilty of a crime.

This gave her hope that he would be free to live a normal life one day. Perhaps he'd even return to teaching. This brought a thought that stirred up unease in her. Would he one day show up to take away the child he sent her?

The wait ate at her, giving her terrible headaches. Her husband called her crazy. She knew that everything would be better when Little Franz was with her.

Her arms ached for her boy. She'd already lost four years with him. All because of Franz's stubborn choice to leave rather than demand Mary give him the child.

She'd whispered and cajoled. After days of tearful entreaties, he finally agreed to pursue Elias Kline.

Tomorrow, Tyson Monroe would leave to begin the search. He was the perfect one to send—a man free from moral constraint and greedy to boot! She'd slyly hinted at possible rewards when he brought her the boy.

Her little Franz. She would have him soon.

CHAPTER 4

Elias Kline changed a few things in his life soon after leaving Mills Bluff. To be on the safe side, as he feared the Sauers would send someone after him to snatch his son, he began to use the name Ezra King. It sounded more American, hinting less of his parents' immigrant status.

The second change he made concerned Frank. He gladly rechristened his son, calling him Buddy King. The boy loved traveling with his father and chattered happily about what he saw as Elias followed the trail from Indiana to Missouri. The new name merely seemed like another part of the adventure. He repeatedly answered to it and could parrot back his new first and last name each time Elias asked him to do so.

Within fifty miles of reaching St. Joseph, he began asking if anyone needed a temporary blacksmith. God opened a door for him in Stewartville. There he met Robbie McDougal who ran a livery and smithy. The man welcomed him with slightly damaged open arms. He pointed to the splinted wrist and told of breaking it a few days before. "Weren't sure what to do, but the Lord above seems to have solved my problem for me."

The man provided a room in his home for Elias and his son. Mrs. McDougal fed them and even did their laundry. It was no stretch to say that they treated him as one of the family to show their appreciation for his work.

While he worked, Mrs. McDougal even watched his son. Part of the day, though, Elias took Buddy with him. He wanted the boy to see him work the forge or care for the horses. It was part of how he would learn to do those things for himself one day.

Working at the smithy, he remembered the day two weeks before that he'd determined to send for a bride. By now the letter would be in the hands of the matchmaker. Surely he'd get a telegram or letter in the mail next week. Would it read that his request was impossible or, God willing, would he learn the name of the woman who would marry him? Thinking about it brought back the memory of the day he wrote the letter.

Buddy had sat on an overturned bucket with a worried frown on his face, watching his father comb burrs from a horse's tail. The little boy's brown curls stuck damply to his forehead from the hot July air.

When he didn't do his usual ceaseless chatter, his father had stopped combing the tail and wiped his sweating forehead with his sleeve. Then he'd prodded the boy. "What's going on in that head of yours? Seems you're deep in thought over there."

Frown still in place, Buddy met his father's gaze. "Do you think Mrs. McDougal would let me call her ma?" Once he asked that question, the boy stuck his thumb in his mouth, reminding Elias of how young the boy was.

At that moment, Elias knew he couldn't put off writing the letter. Even in Mills Bluff, he recognized that he and Buddy would need a woman in their lives. Well, this proved it.

Moving from the rear of the large Percheron, he hung the curry comb on the wall. Once he reached his son, he hoisted the boy into his arms. "She's not your mother. But you need one. I'm going to see to it that we get a new mother for you and a wife for me."

Buddy grinned. "I sure will be glad when she gets here. I want one that will sing to me at night like Mikey's does." The reference to the boy's friend in Mills Bluff surprised Elias. It wasn't the mention of the boy that amazed him. No, it was the fact that, by Buddy's words, he showed his own mother had been lacking. Elias hadn't known that the boy realized what a poor mother Mary had been.

Tenderly patting the boy's back, he then set him down again. "Sit back on your bucket," he instructed. Elias thought the boy was safest if he stayed in that spot while he watched his father work with the animals. When it was time to feed them, Buddy helped give hay and grain. It bothered him a bit that his son appeared much more interested in the care of the horses than in the smithy. Hopefully, he would grow out of that and want to work the metal someday.

At that moment, a thought tickled his mind. If he married again, there might be another son who would work the smithy if Buddy failed to take an interest in learning the trade. He could one day have a livery run by Buddy and a smithy worked by himself and this yet-to-be-born boy.

With that thought in mind, he determined to write that night. He'd send the letter to the matrimonial agency in the morning. After clipping the advertisement from the newspaper a few weeks ago, he'd tucked it among his things to refer to when he got around to sending for a wife. That time had finally come.

Now, a few weeks had passed and he wondered who might come into their lives. Would the agency be able to find a woman to meet all of his requirements?

Outside the livery, he could hear McDougal speaking with someone. As much as possible he allowed the man to deal with customers, staying to the shadows. Since he stood in the stall nearest the door, he easily heard the man's questions as the two moved closer to him.

"If you haven't got anything to hide, there's no reason to deny me. Just a quick look over your horse flesh. After all, my employer deserves to regain his horses if you've got them here."

The burr that typically was absent from his boss' voice made an appearance. In a voice filled with ire, McDougal challenged, "And what keeps you from saying one of my beasties is belonging to your man? Like as not, you're trying to take me stock. Rob me blind, you will."

Elias could easily imagine the tall, heavily muscled man looming over the stranger as he spoke. Putting an eye to a crack between the boards, he waited until the stranger moved. When the man shifted, Elias' hands fisted. It was Tyson Monroe, a man who worked for the Sauer family. That half-moon scarring his face's right side proved his identity.

Had Sauer sent Tyson to accuse him of stealing horses? The team here had belonged to his in-laws, but Elias didn't have paperwork to prove that. Maybe he should write them, as John Smith of course, and ask for a document transferring ownership of them to him.

At least the team wasn't in the livery that day. He'd rented them yesterday to a local man who needed to make a trip into St. Joseph. For the last few weeks, he'd been selectively renting them to make extra money. McDougal had refused to take any of the money Elias earned by doing it. The man and his wife were fast becoming like family. It was no wonder Buddy had wanted to call her ma.

Focusing on the conversation outside, he listened as Tyson described his team of Belgians. McDougal's voice lost its angry tone, becoming carefully neutral instead. The man recognized Elias' team from the description. "Are you saying you have a paper to prove their ownership?"

Tyson looked away as he answered. Maybe his fidgeting would betray what he said as a lie to McDougal. Elias hated to think that the man might believe Tyson Monroe.

"No, I'm trying to find the horses. Nothing else. The boss will come here if we find them. He wants to take care of the man personally." Tyson gave a menacing laugh after he finished speaking.

When the livery owner invited Tyson to examine his horses, Elias quickly climbed into the loft filled with fresh hay. He laid flat on his stomach against the outside wall. As the man moved from stall to stall, Elias heard him ask about Buddy.

"Don't suppose you've seen anything of a large man and a boy? The man's got sort of wheat-colored hair and the boy has brown curls."

"What you want them for?" Suspicion gave his boss' voice a low, menacing sound.

Unable to watch them, Elias had to imagine the other man's shrug. Tyson didn't answer. Neither man spoke for several minutes.

McDougal's indignation was clear when he broke the silence. "There. You've seen them all. Go with you now and leave me to my work."

Without thanking him, the sound of the door closing signaled Tyson's departure. Elias rose and made his way down from the loft.

The older man waited for him at the foot of the ladder. Elias searched his face for some sign of suspicion or accusation. Instead, he saw only curiosity. "Thought you must be up there. Why are you hiding from that man? Didn't figure you to be on the run."

Shaking his head, Elias assured him, "I'm not. At least not on the run from the law. I mean to keep my son, though." Then the story of what he'd lived through in the last two months came pouring out.

Using his good hand, the older man slapped him on the back in a show of solidarity. "We'll not let the parents of such a man take your boy!"

They spoke for a bit and decided that he was safe so far. Tyson hadn't turned up any information on him so the man would move on to another town.

Something worried Elias so he made a suggestion. "Do you suppose I could leave the team here, with you. Swap them out for your

Clydesdales? After all, Tyson may have planted the idea in someone's head that the Belgians are stolen. That person might not take my word that the horses aren't stolen."

With a grin, McDougal sat on a hay bale and motioned for him to do the same. "I've a better plan than that, laddie. Let me tell you what I think would be best."

McDougal had been right. Elias didn't want to lose his well-matched team of Belgians. They were younger and more valuable than the Clydesdales. So, when he'd received the telegram with Miss Hastings' name and arrival date, he put a plan into action.

The day before she arrived, Elias traveled to St. Joseph. When they left their kind hosts, large tears coursed down Buddy's face and he begged Mrs. McDougal to come with them. His father's reassurance that, the very next day, they would get a mother to love Buddy helped stop the boy's tears. Even with that comforting promise, he sucked his thumb for much of the trip to St. Joseph.

As a part of the plan, they stopped outside of the town. McDougal knew a family who lived close to the town. He sent a letter of introduction along with Elias. This kept him away from hotels and liveries where someone might have heard the false information about him.

The farmer and his wife, the Fergusons, appeared overjoyed that he and his son stopped by their place for the night. Their small tribe of children soon pulled a shy Buddy away from his father with the promise of puppies.

While he and Liam Ferguson rubbed down the horses who now stood in clean stalls and munched on clover hay, the man asked about Elias' problem. "Says in the letter you're running to keep your son."

Trusting the man since he was Robbie McDougal's cousin, he allowed his story to come tumbling out. At the end of his retelling, Elias looked at Ferguson with a red face. He didn't usually bare his soul to strangers and certainly never talked that much.

Ferguson wore a thoughtful expression and seemed oblivious to the other man's embarrassment. "By St. Andrew, I think I see some hope. If you'll write down your story, I'll send it to Collin, my brother. True and he owes me a favor or three."

Confused, Elias dropped the hoof he'd been cleaning with a hoof pick and waited for his host to explain his plan. When he only moved to check the hooves on the horse he cared for, Elias nudged him for details.

"How can your brother help me protect my son?"

Satisfied that no dirt or stones were lodged in the hooves, Liam left the stall and stood in front of his guest. "Finished? We can find a better spot to gab than the horse shed. Come along and I'll tell ye about my brother, the U.S. marshal."

Later that evening, Elias sat alone after the children had gone to bed. Quiet settled over the farmhouse and he worked at the library table in the small parlor. The pencil flew across the page similar to a shuttle in a loom and the story of Mary and her lover Franz took shape in front of him. What a stooge he'd been and all because she pursued him, made him think she was interested in him.

Perhaps Collin Ferguson would see clues in what he wrote. As a marshal, he had the training to make sense of crimes like the deaths of Mary and Franz. That night he would pray the man had time in his schedule to go to Mills Bluff or at least that he would send another marshal to investigate.

Remembering his quick marriage to an eager Mary, he promised himself not to be taken in so easily this time. He would show the woman he married—Ruby Hastings—love by providing for her, respecting her role as wife and mother, and giving her children. He might love her with his body, but he'd keep a part of him out of her reach for a time. The past had proven that he fell in love too easily. He wouldn't have his heart broken again.

CHAPTER 5

Shifting nervously, Elias stood on the platform and waited for his bride. He'd left Buddy with the Fergusons. The boy had played with other children so seldom that he begged to stay another day with them. As he'd borrowed Liam Ferguson's team to make the trip into St. Joseph, he'd planned to return there anyhow and gladly let his son stay with them while he made the trip alone.

Liam had gone along with the plan to use his team of Percherons rather than risk someone recognizing Elias' horses at the station. Elias snorted at the thought that he used another man's animals to hide his horses which, actually, weren't his but were really the Schmidts' horses. His life had begun to read like a badly written dime novel!

Peals from a bell sounded the approach of the train. He leaned over the tracks and sighted the gleam of the engine. Seeing its approach started a swarm of locusts in his gut. She was on the train.

He knew she would come. The Lord had blessed every part of his adventure so far and wouldn't allow him to be shamed now by a bride who refused to honor her promise.

The Lord not allowing him to be ashamed? Where had that thought come from? In his life before the war, he'd often repeated James 5:16, clinging to it as a lifeline even as his faith ebbed and had all but ceased after Gettysburg. *The effectual fervent prayers of a righteous man availeth much.*

He prayed because he had been taught it as a habit. Now, he wondered if anyone heard his petition.

Regardless of his doubts, he'd wanted religion for his son. Even when his wife fought him about it, they'd attended church. As soon as his son could speak, Elias began to teach him short verses. His parents had done the same with him and it had stood him well through the tribulations of his marriage and then the tumult of the last two months. Whether God existed or not, he wanted those same values taught to his son. If that made him a hypocrite, well, he didn't care.

Steam brought his mind back to the train. He stepped back from the edge of the platform and away from the hot vapors belched out by the engine. As it began to lessen, he saw a figure emerge from the temporary mist. She glided toward him with the elegance of a duchess. Her dark green traveling suit outlined an enticing figure as she confidently made her way in his direction.

Elias checked behind him to see who the attractive woman could be approaching. He saw no one in back of him. Could this dark-haired beauty possibly be his bride?

She stopped in front of him and tipped her head up to smile. Soft brown eyes met his own blue ones, and he reminded himself not to fall in love.

"Mr. King?" Her distinctly eastern syllables sounded exotic, definitely alluring. He memorized her face as if imprinting it on his brain. He'd seen prettier women, his first wife for one. This one's calm and confidence drew him. Looking at her, he sensed a helpmate who would take on life with an easy assurance.

Suddenly he realized his mouth hung open. Embarrassed, he closed it and cleared his throat. During his rude inspection, she hadn't fidgeted or lost the peaceful air. She impressed him.

"Yes, that's me. Miss Hastings, I hope." His deep voice rose a bit as he spoke.

Under the upturned brim of her wide hat, her eyes wrinkled at the corners as she gave a tinkle of laughter. "I'm glad you want that to be me. You studied me so closely I thought you might be disappointed."

Disappointed? Relieved described his mood. She'd arrived, the epitome thus far of all he'd asked for in his letter. Opening his mouth, he intended to tell her that before a railway worker approached and cut him off.

"Excuse me, Mrs., but I got to get on to other things. Those crates and trunks are off to the side over yonder." He pointed to what Elias thought must be a shipment of goods for one of the local businesses. "You'll need to take your basket now, unless you're wanting me to find a porter to carry her."

With a gracious smile, Miss Hastings handed the man a coin and took hold of the basket's handle. It was overly large and a thin blanket draped across the handle and over the top, concealing the contents.

"Odd, that man calling you missus rather than miss." He'd cocked a dark blonde eyebrow at her, wondering if his question would crack her calm composure.

Before answering, his bride pulled back an edge of the blanket. Peeking at the contents, she smiled.

The smile confused Elias. It wasn't the type of expression a person wore if everything was as it should be. Really, the smile reminded him of how he grinned at his son.

Prickles ran down his spine and he reached out to claim her basket. "Let me take that. It looks heavy and awkward." He placed a hand beside hers, brushing her fingers with his own.

A spark passed between them at the touch. Amazed, he looked at her. Her face showed astonishment as well. With no fuss, she allowed him to claim her burden.

This was new to him. He'd been attracted to Mary, true. There'd never been the flash of strong attraction he'd just felt. Good thing the wedding was arranged for that afternoon.

The woman—his woman—came to her senses and realized she no longer held the basket. "No, I can take it. Please, I'd rather you handle the carpetbags." Her eyes and tip of her head pointed his gaze back to the mountain of crates. Her bags must be over there. She didn't mention the crates. Perhaps that meant they weren't hers, after all.

Offering her his arm, he turned to take her to claim the carpetbags. As he did so, the basket jostled gently against his leg. A soft squeal sounded from beneath the blanket.

Elias froze. Miss Hastings stumbled slightly at his sudden stop. Her eyes asked a question. Another cry from the basket changed that question to a look of resignation.

"I'd hoped to be away from here before I told you about her. Could we perhaps sit down in the depot's waiting room to talk?" She met his eyes directly. Nothing in her look indicated guilt or deception.

Commenting with a silent nod, he led her into the station's main room and to a bench positioned against the far wall. It promised the most privacy for their talk.

Waiting for her to sit down, he followed. Sitting close to her, he angled his body on the shiny polished wood. He needed to watch her face as she spoke.

Instead of beginning her explanation, she removed the blanket and lifted out a pink-cheeked infant. Tufts of blonde hair stood on end, like down on a baby chick. The infant's mouth had formed a round "oh" as she blinked at the sunlight. Then she turned her gaze to Elias and smiled.

His arms went out for her in an action as automatic as breathing. She drew him to her as easily as Ruby Hastings had. Ruby released the infant to him and her weight in his arms reassured him. It was a feeling of coming home. While it made no sense to him, he felt the same as when he'd first held his newborn son.

The blue-eyed girl stuffed a fist into her rosebud mouth and stared back at him. Then she rested her cheek trustingly against his chest and closed her eyes with a sigh. Not even the wet diaper disturbed the magic of that moment for him.

In a soft and even voice, Miss Hastings explained. Not Miss Hastings—Ruby. He would marry her and keep both of them. The peace that folded around him in the presence of these two made that decision for him.

"I've raised children for the last nineteen years. My mother died giving birth to my sister. With the help of a cook, I kept house for my father and took care of my brother and the baby." She laid a hand on his arm. He thought the touch was meant as an appeal. It sparked longing in him, reminding him that they had a wedding to get to and would need to leave soon.

At the sensations, she blushed and lowered her eyes. "This baby arrived a day before I planned to leave. Her mother died and my brother can't care for her."

The baby wasn't hers? He wanted to blurt out the question but stopped himself. What did it matter? He was keeping them, even if she hadn't fit his requirement of an unmarried woman.

Instead, he stroked the baby's dandelion fluff and asked, "What's her name?"

She ran a finger along the sleeping baby's cheek and smiled. "Letty Louise Hastings."

Her motion reinforced his belief that this woman would be a good mother to Buddy. She would see the boy's need for love, he hoped, and reach out to his son.

"You know from my letter I've not been using my real name. A minister is waiting for us. He'll marry us proper with my real name since I can trust him." Pausing, he watched her bob her head but not say anything.

"The thing is, we need to leave soon to meet with him. We'll marry and then go to raising this little one—" He leaned down and placed a light kiss to the baby's head. "—along with my boy."

Glowing with joy at his words, she smiled and nodded. He was quickly discovering that she was a woman of few words. Maybe that would change as she grew comfortable with him.

His heart sank when she finally spoke. "We have to make arrangements for my crates."

No! Please, dear God, let her answer no. "You don't mean that mountain of boxes to one side of the platform."

Ignoring any distress in his voice, she calmly answered. "Yes, I've brought household goods and some items of furniture with me. Along with my trunks, of course."

Running his free hand down his face, he groaned. "Didn't you understand we're traveling by wagon? How am I supposed to move all those crates when we'll already be loaded down with supplies and the like?" Hopefully, she would see how impossible it would be to haul her boxes with them.

Those soft brown eyes held a pleading look, even though her voice remained calm and matter of fact. "If we follow the old Oregon Trail, the train will be close by. I plan to keep sending my goods forward on it. They'll be stored until we arrive in the town." A measuring glance in his direction assessed his reaction. When he only nodded, she went on with the same tone. "If we choose not to settle nearby, the crates will be shipped ahead on the line, to another town. I've money enough to do that and consider it my dowry."

Her forethought fascinated him. She was unlike the women he'd known. Practical to be a help in setting up a home and business, and yet, she was purely feminine and appealing at the same time.

"Sounds like you've planned it out. Let's speak to them at the ticket counter about sending the crates on. Then we have a wedding to get to."

"Now, I understand this is an arranged marriage. A man needs a woman to help him build a life out west." The silver-haired minister stopped speaking to throw a smile in his own wife's direction. The plump, white-haired woman looked up from Letty and blew a kiss to her husband. He pretended to catch it. Their silliness delighted Ruby.

When he continued, his voice held a different, very grave tone. "But, even when a couple doesn't have a love match, I am charged by the Lord to remind them about God's definition of a right and proper marriage."

Ruby looked up at Ezra King. Or was it Elias Kline? This game of fake names confused her. Still, she trusted him to fully explain it later. Now, she was satisfied with the feeling of rightness that settled on her when near the man. She'd prayed about this union and believed this peace and sense of rightness came directly from the Holy Spirit.

The man was incredibly handsome. His dark blonde hair waved, curling at the very ends around his neck. His icy blue eyes were anything but cold as they looked down at her. His glance made her forget that she was an undesirable, mousy spinster. For the first time in her life, she thought someone might find her attractive. That feeling was almost as nice as the ripples of sensation his touch created.

The somber-voiced minister opened his bible and read to them. "The fifth chapter of Ephesians has a lot to teach about marriage. *Husbands, love your wives, even as Christ also loved the church and gave himself for it.* Elias Kline, will you love this woman? Will you be faithful to her, provide and protect her, and be the spiritual head of your house?"

With confidence ringing in his baritone voice, her groom agreed. "I do."

Ruby expected the minister to turn to her, but he wasn't finished with Elias. "If you love her, she will love you back. Most women are made that way. They respond to love and protection. It's why God told husbands to love them. He didn't have to command the women to love their husbands. It just naturally seems to follow."

The man's glance turned to Ruby then. "Now, Ruby Hastings, will you honor and respect this man? Will you be faithful to him and endure the trials of life by his side?"

When she opened her mouth to speak, nothing came out. A lump of emotion clogged her voice. Alarmed at her silence, Elias looked down at her and squeezed her hand, probably trying to prompt her answer. Finally, she whispered a soft, "I will." She grinned as her husband visibly relaxed. How could he believe she'd pass up the chance to marry his handsome self?

"You agreed to respect him. Trials in life and arguments might come up that make that a challenge. Still, the bible is clear on this." Here the minister read from his bible. "*Nevertheless let everyone of you in particular so love his wife even as himself; and the wife see that she reverence her husband.* You respect him, honor his decisions. He's made so that your respect deepens his love for you."

The man studied them, allowing his words to sink in. Evidently whatever he saw in their faces pleased him because he grinned broadly and said, "I now pronounce you man and wife. If you want—

and I'd recommend it—you may now kiss your bride."

Ducking his head under her hat's wide brim, Elias' lips pressed tenderly against hers. Soft and persuasive, his lips teased hers before pulling away. His grin at her dreamy expression showed that she'd pleased him.

After the ceremony, the preacher and his wife invited them to stay for a lunch of coffee and sandwiches. She expected him to be in a hurry to leave. Maybe because he'd been in a hurry to get the marriage done. She'd believed they were headed out that night to get his son.

So it surprised her when he agreed to eat with the older couple. Then Elias lingered over coffee and shared stories from the war. She'd heard tales from the men who'd returned to her home town. They told stories of gruesome battles. Her husband somehow managed to have funny stories from that horrible war. She considered what this told her about him.

"Mrs. Kline?"

Ruby started at the use of the name. Elias had told the minister and his wife his real name. That wasn't what startled her, though. Hearing herself called by a new name surprised her.

She looked at Mrs. Parker and realized the minister's wife waited for her response. The woman must have asked her a question and she'd missed it while she considered Elias' war stories.

Ruby turned her attention away from her husband and smiled apologetically. "I'm sorry. Did you ask something?"

"I wondered if you wanted to bathe Letty and dress her for bed. I have warm water ready." Bless this woman! She knew they'd traveled for days by train. Poor Letty would benefit from being clean.

Retrieving the carpetbag from under the seat of Elias' wagon—she needed to think of him as Eli— Ruby entered the small house and returned to the kitchen. Mrs. Parker and the baby were gone. Following the splashing sounds, she found them outside on the small porch.

The woman supported Letty's head with one hand and ran a cloth over the little back with her other one. Small legs and arms thrashed at the water. When water splashed onto her face, Letty froze and whimpered. Mrs. Parker clucked reassuringly to her and ran the rag over the infant's downy head.

Fishing a gown and two diapers out of the bag, Ruby dropped them onto a wooden table pushed up against outside of the house. As the older woman lifted the baby from the tin tub, she held up the towel laying near it and wrapped her niece. Rubbing the blonde hair, she leaned down and breathed in her sweet baby smell.

Placing Letty on the table, Ruby placed two squares of cotton flannel together, double-diapering her for the night. With added protection and since she was exhausted from their travel, Letty should sleep most of the night.

"Thank you for letting me bathe her. I used to love that time with my children." The woman paused as if considering something important. Then she continued speaking. "I wanted to add something to what my husband told you about the recipe for a good marriage."

Tying Letty's gown closed, Ruby raised the baby to her shoulder and gave Mrs. Parker her attention. Ruby felt the curiosity that gleamed from her own eyes as she waited for the woman to continue.

The woman lowered her voice, speaking confidentially. "It's a secret an older woman told me when I married. When you don't agree with your husband, start praying that the good Lord will show him how wrong he is. With a husband who's a believer, this works so much of the time and allows you to honor both your spouse and your God."

Grinning at the woman's solution to marital problems, Ruby thanked her before changing the subject. "Will you direct me to a nearby place to buy canned milk and corn syrup? I need it to make Letty's bottles tomorrow."

Looking at her oddly, Mrs. Parker gave her directions to a mercantile. "But why didn't you nurse your daughter?"

The question started a warm glow in Ruby. The older lady believed her to be Letty's mother and the thought pleased Ruby no end.

"I'm actually her aunt," she said as before explaining about Letty's mother. It was wonderful to pretend she was the baby's mother. At the back of her mind, though, lurked the thought of her brother returning to take Letty away.

CHAPTER 6

A touch on her shoulder jerked Ruby awake. In the dim light, she groggily focused on the face in front of her. Her husband smiled at her. When her eyes moved from his face to his bare chest, she whipped the blankets over her head.

His chuckle intensified her embarrassment, proving he was more comfortable with this part of marriage than she was. Lowering the blanket an inch, she peeked over its edge to see him buttoning up his cambric shirt.

He noticed her and grinned. "Good. You've emerged!" He moved to the bed and pulled the blanket down a little further to give her a lingering kiss. "Letty's stirring so I'm headed downstairs to see if they'll warm up her morning bottle."

With the full bottle in his right hand, he made as if to open the door. Then he surprised her by returning to the bed for one more kiss. Stroking one finger down her cheek, he whispered, "Good morning, Mrs. Kline."

The emotion of the situation made her shy. Ducking her head, she hoped teasing him might erase some of this feeling she had when he was so near. "That's Mrs. King, now. Remember that, sir."

Elias let out a short bark of laughter that brought a cry from Letty. The man was certainly in a good mood this morning, Ruby observed. She blushed at the thought that the past night might have something to do with his excellent humor.

After the door closed behind him, she pulled her nightgown over her head and moved across the cold wooden floor to Letty's basket. The baby's rosebud mouth puckered in distress, ready to cry again. Recognizing Ruby leaning over her, the little one's mouth quickly changed into a smile and she kicked her legs vigorously, almost upsetting her wicker basket.

Those strong movements were the reason Ruby had placed the basket on the floor rather than on the table near the tall window. In her mind, she'd imagined the baby rolling off the table during the night. Still, the floor was cold so she picked the basket up and moved it to the middle of the bed for now.

Would there be some way to haul a cradle with them as they traveled westward? As she lifted the wet infant from it she realized that even a box would make a better bed for the three-month-old than this basket.

Thankfully, the evening before she'd been able to buy more flannel. Letty had gone through her supply of clean diapers. While Ruby had rinsed them in Mrs. Clark's tub, using a bar of lye soap and the baby's still-warm bathwater, those diapers were outside on the hotel's clothesline. Right now, she wiped the baby's bottom and put one of the new squares of white flannel on her.

With her bottom now dry and in a fresh sack securely tied at the bottom, Letty cooed and waved her hands while Ruby sang hymns for her. Ruby needed to dress for the day and drew a brown calico out of her bag. Its cheery flower pattern might distract people from the mess of wrinkles it had become while packed.

Sighing, she supposed she ought to wear the outfit Elias bought her. Last evening at the mercantile, he'd selected the flounced and shortened skirt and held it up to her as he extolled its advantages. He meant well, but the skirt's hemline seemed so--well—scandalous. After all, if she didn't wear the tall boots, a man would be able to see her ankles. Calling it a prairie skirt, Elias had explained that she'd need the shorter skirt as they traveled west. Well, they weren't starting that journey today, so she would wear her terribly wrinkled dress!

There was no dressing screen to hide behind. She hurriedly removed her nightgown. With her petticoat and chemise donned, she grimaced as she considered the corset. How she hated the thing, but without it, her bosom lacked support. With a sigh of resignation, she fitted it around her waist.

As she began to tug on the laces, the bedroom door opened. With a gasp of alarm, she dropped the laces and snatched up her brown calico to hold in front of herself. One night of intimacy couldn't erase a lifetime of modesty.

At her unease, Elias kept his gaze pointedly away from her and moved to the wriggling baby on the bed. "Come here, Letty girl. I've got something for you."

Settling in a chair placed by the table, he sat down and offered the bottle to the infant. Like a baby bird, she opened her mouth and sucked strongly at the rubber nipple. Ruby stood mesmerized by the scene of this large, muscled man cradling her tiny niece.

"She sure is hungry. Amazing that she wasn't screaming her heart out for the bottle." He laughed at the baby's enthusiastic nursing and leaned down to kiss her blonde fluff that, as usual, stood straight up on her small head.

His words woke Ruby from the spell. Turning away to finish tying her corset, she then pulled the dress over her head before answering him. "She's very patient, just like her mother. I see a lot of Alicia in the baby, though her features resemble my brother."

"Was his wife's name Alicia?" He glanced her way when he asked the question and didn't look away when he saw her button up her dress.

Ruby fidgeted a bit under his gaze and mentally decided to stop being silly and accept the intimacy that came with the close quarters of marriage. With a calm she coached herself to feel, she answered, "Yes, the poor dear's gone now. I worry, though, about growing to love Letty and then losing her to my brother."

"We can adopt her. Claim she was abandoned." He spoke with a firmness that rejected any point of view other than his own.

Using a coaxing voice that dripped with false cheer, she reasoned with him. "You wouldn't want to lose your boy just because his mother is dead. I fear it's the same for my brother. We can't consider Letty ours forever."

Elias knew he had paled at her words. Without knowing his story, she decided something she said hit close to home with him.

Clearing his throat, she watched him struggle to explain. "Uh, yep. You're right 'bout that. I'm running from people who think they should raise him."

Ruby narrowed her eyes. "Why? Does this have to do with folks calling you a murderer?"

Putting Letty's blanket over his shoulder, he laid the little girl on it and gently patted until she burped loudly. Returning her to the cradle of his arms, he offered her the bottle again.

That done, he smiled at Ruby before answering her question. "It's sort of about that. The day after my wife drowned, a man named Franz Sauer was found dead, shot."

He kept his eyes fixed on her face as he talked, something liars rarely did to Ruby's way of thinking. "Some folks think I killed Sauer and now his parents want Buddy. After all, most everyone in Mills Bluff knows he fathered my son."

Clever Tyson Monroe! He'd found Elias Kline.

"Ezra King!" Her mouth twisted as she said the name. The man was willing to give up a fine German name to hide a boy that wasn't his. That proved he shouldn't be allowed to raise her Franz.

She stood outside the opened window to hear the men. Tyson, with his annoying oily voice, boasted of finding them. He'd asked what his employer wanted him to do.

Tonight, she would visit Tyson and explain how to use men who were willing to kill for a small amount of money.

CHAPTER 7

She sat alone in the wagon. Well, alone except for Letty who slept peacefully in her basket. Ruby glanced at her and shooed a fly away from the baby's sweet face.

Elias had parked the wagon in an alley, at the backdoor of the mercantile they'd visited yesterday. The store owner had agreed to keep their order until the morning, agreeing it would be safer in his backroom than in the hotel's livery. Her husband had left the wagon and headed inside to let the man know they'd arrived to pick it up.

Watching his back disappear around the corner of the building, Ruby thought back to his comment. How could he casually remark that someone else fathered his child? And the true father's parents wanted the child?

No, not a true father. She refused to believe that a physical act that created a child was solely responsible for making that man the father. From the tender way he spoke about the boy, she knew that Elias deeply loved his son. Someone wanted Elias to be thought of as a murderer so he'd lose his child.

Another thought came to mind as she sat there. If he so easily parented another man's child, it was no wonder he willingly accepted Letty. The man truly loved children. That morning, while she'd dressed and tidied the hotel room, he'd crooned to the baby and played peekaboo with her as if she was his own. Remembering it brought a warmth and contentment that filled her.

"Pssst!" The sound jerked her out of her memories.

Glancing around, Ruby saw a dark bowler hat just above the back corner of the wagon. The head it sat on raised, and she gasped.

"Onie!" At her loud cry, he scowled and held a finger to his lips. With an answering scowl, she whispered, "What are you doing here?"

He moved around the wagon and stood near her. "Anna told me your message so I figured which train you'd take to get here. I've been traveling on the same train with you since Pennsylvania. I even followed you yesterday so I know you married the man you're with now."

His choice of words made Ruby sound like a hussy who spent time with various men and had finally married one. She ignored that and hissed out an accusation. "You followed me, but never tried to talk with me? Are you that afraid because of those posters?" Since she'd sent a plea for help to Emmie's father-in-law, Ruby had put the bounty on Onyx's head out of her mind, as if the matter had been resolved. Or, maybe, she'd been so involved with Letty and the worries about her future.

Onyx waved a hand to dismiss her question and leaned close to her face. "We have something more important to talk about, Ruby."

She expected he wanted to discuss his daughter. What he said came as a surprise.

"I think you need to convince your husband to take me along with you. I stood outside the hotel watching for you this morning, sort of hiding in the shadows. Then I heard three men discussing your man."

He stopped, an actor surveying his audience as his gaze searched her face. Onie always had a flair for the dramatic. She exaggerated her look of curiosity to encourage him.

Before continuing, his gaze checked the alley to be sure they were still alone. "The one they called Tyson, a short man with an evil squint, said they could come up with something to accuse Elias Kline with and to go ahead and shoot him if they were sure it was him."

This time she didn't feign a reaction. Horror filled her. "They plan to kill my husband? Why?"

Onie fixed an expression of sorrow on his face and put a hand to his chin as if in thought. His blue eyes, though, snapped with energy and enjoyment. Ruby wanted to pinch him. Why, her brother acted as if he was enjoying this.

Drawing out his words, he finally answered her. "I only know that someone named Sauer wants Kline's boy."

Snorting, Ruby dismissed him with a wave. "We already know that. Didn't you hear anything else?"

Onie scrunched up his face in thought. She thought he looked desperate for something to say that might shock or alarm her. Idly, she considered that he must be an interesting teacher since he craved an audience's reactions.

Shaking his head sadly, he repeated his earlier words. "Nothing else. I just know that they're willing to kill your husband to get his son."

"Who's after my boy?" A voice boomed those words and a large hand settled on Onie's shoulder.

Elias managed to alarm both of them since both had been lost in their conversation. "Well, tell me who you are and what you know about a threat to my boy," he demanded in a cold voice.

Turning to face him, Onie visibly swallowed and looked up into the much taller man's face.

"Some man named Tyson and two others. I heard them talking this morning outside the hotel."

Narrowing his eyes, Elias stared at Onie. He managed to shock Ruby again with his next words. "You must be Ruby's brother."

With an effort, her brother closed his mouth which gaped open in surprise. Then he asked, "What makes you think that?"

Shrugging, Elias answered but didn't remove his heavy hand from Onie's shoulder. "I just spent an hour tending to a little girl who has the same features as you. Makes sense that you have to be her father."

"Yeah, she's mine. I followed them out here. With a bounty on my head, I needed to move on anyhow."

The mention of a bounty had Elias' eyebrows arching upward. His gaze went to Ruby with a look that said he would demand an explanation once they were alone. Then he held out his hand to Onie.

"Ezra King's the name I go by. And you?" His question implied that he expected to hear an alias.

Shaking the other man's hand, Onie smiled and answered, "John Johnson's the name. Nice to meet you, Mr. King. You have a lovely wife and daughter in that wagon. How about I come along and help you protect them?"

Buddy was the target! He'd known the Sauers wanted to somehow get ahold of his boy, but he'd expected them to have him arrested and tried. That they would use legal means to get rid of him and claim the boy as his guardians.

And what about the Schmidts? Did the Sauers think Mary's parents wouldn't protest or try to claim him for themselves?

None of this made sense. And now, if he swallowed his brother-in-law's story, Tyson had given the okay to grab his son. Had that been Mr. Sauer's idea or was Tyson doing whatever he thought expedient to please his employer?

His wife sat stiffly beside him. From her posture, either she was upset or she hadn't ridden often in wagons. Her fingers held tightly to the board seat with her brows wrinkled in distress or concentration. He didn't know her well enough yet to decide which.

So far his spinster bride pleased him mightily. He sensed the will and strength in her to face the problems threatening them. Too, she didn't show any shock when he'd revealed the truth about Buddy's beginnings. He liked her calm demeanor.

The only time she'd appeared genuinely surprised was when they met the Ferguson family at the sheriff's office. The fact that they'd arrived at the jail didn't seem to bother her. What threw her off-kilter was his mention of heading out on the trail after speaking to the sheriff. At least he hoped they would.

From a distance, he recognized the Ferguson family. Liam Ferguson and his crowd met them outside the jail. Buddy jumped from the back of the covered wagon and straight into his arms as he pulled alongside the other vehicle.

"Whoa there boy! You about got under the wagon wheels and scared a year off of me!" He cuddled his son against him while scolding him.

The brown curls cuddled against his shoulder, Buddy's face hidden in his neck. "I knew you'd catch me, Daddy. It's just I got so happy inside when I saw you it felt like I could fly."

A lump formed in Elias' throat and he leaned down to kiss his boy's head, not saying anything. On the bench next to him, Ruby cleared her throat. He looked at her and caught her pointing at his son.

"Buddy, look at me, son." When the boy raised his head, Elias smiled at him. "I've got someone for you to meet. Two someones actually."

"She's my new ma, isn't she? My ma came!" Buddy's face took on a glow of excitement as he studied Ruby. "Are you going to be a nice ma?"

She laughed softly at that. "I hope so, but I will expect you to obey." She reached a hand out to his face and laid it on his cheek softly. "Still, I think we will have many wonderful times together."

A squeak let them know that Letty was awake. Probably had been since the wagon stopped. Elias marveled at how easy going the child was. Her father bristled with energy and yet this child seemed to have inherited a naturally easy-going temperament.

"What's that noise, Pa?" Buddy peeked at the covered basket sitting on the floor of the wagon by Ruby's feet. She pulled back the blanket and the boy's mouth formed an oh.

"There's your new cousin, son. She's living with us for a while." Elias watched his son's reaction. He hadn't been around many babies. Mary had lost every child they'd conceived together so Buddy didn't have siblings—yet.

His son's expression showed that this was all a great adventure to him. He bounced off of his father's lap and kneeled by the baby, holding out a finger for her to take. Gurgling joyfully, Letty gripped his finger before she tried to pull it into her mouth.

Pulling his finger away, Buddy chortled. "She thinks my finger's food, Daddy. Did you see she was gonna eat it?"

Laughing, Ruby explained, "She likes to chew on things but won't eat you. We need to give her a toy to gum, instead." She reached into the baby's basket and pulled out the rattle they purchased yesterday. Putting the wooden handle into Letty's hand, she helped the baby grip it and then shook it so that the beads hit against the red metal top. Letty's eyes widened. Then she grasped it on her own, struggling to shake it. Buddy took over, helping her rattle it.

Reaching out, Elias gripped his wife's hand gently. "Just what I thought. They'll be fast friends." She smiled at him and squeezed his much larger hand in agreement.

"Now, let me introduce these folks to you." He'd stopped the wagon, the brake already set. Stepping out, he reached in and lifted Ruby down, hands lingering on her waist as if they had a mind of their own. She stepped around and lifted the baby from her basket. Buddy climbed down after them, running back to the Ferguson children.

He heard his son's call to "come meet my new ma and the baby," joy bubbling up inside of Elias at the good turn the Westward Home and Hearts

Agency had done him. Now he just needed to find a home for them in a small, out of the way town.

Elias shook hands with Liam before introducing Ruby to the couple. He focused again on the man then. "Thanks for getting a top on it. Did I give you enough money for it?"

The man fished in his pocket and pulled out a few coins. "Oh aye, plenty for the job and a few coppers left over. We'll just put yer things in and speak to the sheriff. The wife is wanting to get to the store and back home right quick-like."

He looked down at his wife who smiled apologetically. She nodded and smiled regretfully. "I've dough raising and wash on the line. So many things to get done with a crowd like mine."

Telling the children to wait in the covered wagon, the adults entered the jail. Providence was with them as the sheriff sat behind his desk. The man rose when the four stepped toward him.

"Names Sheriff Thomas Kidd. How can I help you?" He stroked a dark brown mustache as he took the group's measure before shaking hands with the men as they made their introductions.

Explaining about the trouble in Mills Bluff, Elias then allowed Liam to hand the telegram from his U.S. marshal brother. Collin had sent it, confirming he would head to Mills Bluff and speak with the sheriff there as well as look into the murders.

Sheriff Kidd tipped a face up to take the taller man's measure before nodding. "I'll see to it that anyone trying to turn you in for murder knows about this. Good thing you came to me. Still, I haven't seen any posters."

Elias explained about Tyson and the men who may be gunning for him. Thomas Kidd frowned and nodded his head in understanding, but he said nothing.

When it seemed that the men were finished speaking, Ruby stepped forward. Softly but with confident authority, she brought up the posters that promised a bounty for Onyx Hastings. "My brother has been falsely accused of kidnapping. It's more likely that someone will try to capture him and turn him in."

With an eyebrow raised, Kidd gestured for them to sit and then resumed his seat. "What makes you think the kidnapping was false?"

Ruby gave an indelicate snort. "That giggling girl was all too happy to elope with my brother. I witnessed the wedding myself. It's her father who stirred up the trouble. First, he tried to accuse him of theft, but the law disproved that quick enough. The local sheriff refuses to press kidnapping charges."

Taking a paper out of her reticule, she set it on the empty surface of the oak desk and pushed it toward him. "Here are the names and directions of both the sheriff and the lawyer who is working to send out notices that my brother isn't truly guilty of the crime."

Turning over the paper, the sheriff studied the wanted poster. Then he read the information she'd written on the back of it before raising his brown eyes to her. "Yep, good information to have. Thank you, ma'am."

"You're welcome. I've no idea how far from here we'll settle, but I've an idea any bounty hunter will head back here with my brother if they catch him." She gave a firm nod to emphasize her words and Elias glimpsed the steel that made up the core of this woman. It pleased him mightily.

"That's not the end of it, Mrs. Kline or Mrs. King. Not sure how you plan to go on with your name change." Looking at Elias, the sheriff shrugged after mentioning his multiple names. "I can't just take your word that this Onyx Hastings isn't a criminal. You'd better stay another day in St. Joseph. I'll send off telegrams and then come speak with you both and Mr. Hastings."

Moving his focus to her husband, Sheriff Kidd squared his shoulders as if ready for a battle. "Where will I find you? At the hotel?"

Squinting his eyes, Elias otherwise didn't reveal his displeasure. "Nah, I'm not taking a chance on my team being recognized. Tyson's been putting out a description of my Percherons." With a finger over his mouth in thought, he paused and then suggested, "Guess we'll camp just west of St.

Joseph. Directly west of here, near the river. Good enough?"

With a bob of his head, the sheriff agreed. "Yep, I'll look you up. Hopefully sooner than later. If everything turns out like you said, ma'am," here he looked at Ruby, "I'll do my best to tell the law in the area about Hastings' innocence."

Rising, Elias helped Ruby to her feet. "We won't take up more of your time, Sheriff Kidd. Just wanted to let you know about our circumstances. We're appreciative of any future help you can give us."

Again the men shook hands and then the group silently left. On the street, they exchanged glances before Liam gave Elias' shoulder a companionable slap.

"That's that, I'm thinking. Send us a note where you settle, in case Collin needs to know." His ruddy Scotts face glowed with friendliness and satisfaction at helping them, Elias thought. For all the trouble at leaving his home and an excellent business, he'd been blessed again and again by people like Liam on this trip.

"We will do that. Take care and God bless. You've certainly been a blessing to me and mine." They shook hands and the couple climbed into the wagon Elias had been driving.

Frowning, Mrs. Ferguson handed him Letty's basket with a caution. "Rough times are ahead for you, I fear. Take care that you and your woman are praying together through it since you're starting out strangers."

He nodded to her, mulling over her words. He'd never prayed with Mary. In fact, he wasn't sure the woman ever did pray, except at mealtime. Was Ruby different? Would praying together give him a better marriage than the coldly indifferent one he shared with Mary?

CHAPTER 8

Onyx had been waiting in the alley alongside the jail, already mounted on his chestnut gelding. Once Elias had Ruby in the wagon, he followed behind them.

Letty fussed and Ruby did her best to change her in the moving vehicle. From the back of the wagon, Buddy peered over the seat, making faces at the crying baby until she stopped her noise and watched him. Ruby marveled at it for a moment, amazed by how quickly the two were bonding.

The drive out of St. Joseph went quickly. The jail stood near the western edge of the town, adding to their rapid exit. Seeing a clump of trees in front of them, Ruby tugged on Elias' arm.

"What do you think about that spot? Some cover but not far from the river." If she had to camp, the added shelter of the trees would be welcomed.

Nodding, her husband headed the team in that direction. "Good idea. Handy source for firewood, too."

The mention of firewood stirred a buzz of worry in Ruby's middle. "I've never cooked over anything but the cookstove at home. I'm really not sure how to—" She broke off since any other explanation didn't seem needed.

Her husband gave her a measuring gaze. "Bet you'll get the hang of it in no time. You seem like the kind to stick to something until you can do it."

Well, his confidence in her certainly was satisfying. She determined to watch over anything she cooked until she figured it out. Hopefully, they'd find a home in the next couple weeks and this rough living wouldn't last for long.

After choosing a flat spot at the edge of the trees and, to her disappointment, not under them, Elias stopped the wagon. With Buddy following him, he set up the canvas tent at the side of the wagon. The boy jumped and clapped his hands. He seemed to always be in motion as far as Ruby could tell.

He stopped clapping long enough to ask about the canvas dwelling. "I get to sleep in the tent. We're sleeping together, right Daddy?" Hopeful eyes peered up at his father. Hiding her mouth behind her hand, she stifled a laugh at Elias' grimace. Obviously, he'd planned for the tent to be theirs alone, probably with the kids in the wagon. That wouldn't have worked, though. She didn't plan to be separated from Letty.

Holding Letty, cold wetness let Ruby know that the baby was soaked through and had been wet for a while. "You are such a good-natured girl, but you do make a lot of messes," she teased the little one, jostling her slightly to quiet her fussing as Ruby climbed into the back of the wagon.

Pushing bags and boxes aside, she searched for the baby's second carpetbag. Letty had already messed all of the diapers and gowns packed in the first one and desperately needed what was in the other bag. No matter how many items she shoved aside, Ruby couldn't locate the bag.

In her mind, she saw it tucked under the table in the hotel. *Oh mercy, did I leave it?*

Stepping out of the wagon, she saw that Onie hadn't removed the saddle yet from his mount. "Brother mine, I've forgotten your daughter's bag at the hotel. Ride back in and get it, please."

Her husband held up a hand. "They aren't going to give it to him. Besides, I know which hotel and what room. Seems to me, I'd make you a better champion in this, m'lady." He ended on a teasing tone, almost flirtatious. It was one she'd never heard out of him, but she liked it.

With the sun shining in the smile she directed at him, Ruby stepped to his side. "Definitely right, kind sir. You will be a wonderful champion to take up the quest." Then abandoning their playful banter, she grew serious. "Onie is a crack shot and will protect us well enough until you return. But, hurry back. I have an unhappy wet little miss."

She held the baby up to him and he kissed the downy head before grinning at her. "Yep, I have a lot to return to. I promise, no lollygagging." Swinging up on the gelding, he headed off with a backward wave.

Ruby determined to find something for the baby in the meantime. Looking through boxes, she found tea towels and diapered Letty. Then she laid her out on a woolen blanket to kick her legs. At least the day was still warm and the little one didn't absolutely need anything more than a diaper.

Onie casually glanced at his daughter and then returned his gaze to the horizon. So far, he'd disappointed Ruby with his lack of interest in the baby.

"What are your plans for her, Onie? Is she mine for good or will you take her away someday?"

Lost in thought, he startled at her questions and looked confused. Ruby wondered if he even knew who the "she" was.

She pointed down at the baby. He followed her finger and then shrugged. "Not much a man can do for a baby except to protect and provide. I can help out once I get a job, but I'm not much interested in raising her. Think your husband will keep her?"

Ruby nodded as she stared at her brother, gauging his mood. Was this the grief talking or could he really be that emotionally distant?

"Well, that's good then." Onie turned away to stare east toward St. Joseph. "I figure any trouble will come from that direction. Why don't you gather the wood while I watch camp?"

She held out her hand to Buddy who squatted next to the baby, playing with her toes while she squealed with delight. "Let's get the wood and we can explore that stand of trees while we do it." He jumped up and took it, happy for an adventure.

The grove was sparse. They seemed to be mostly oaks and would make good firewood, she was relieved to note. Anything to make the fire burn better and help her make a meal for them.

While they walked, she smiled down at Buddy. He grinned back at her and pulled on her hand to stop them. "I like you as my new mama. My old mama never smiled at me." After saying that, he dropped her hand and began picking up sticks, pretending that each was a sword as he thrust it in front of him at an imaginary enemy.

What was she like? Buddy's words had her wondering about the woman she'd already replaced. She had come west to help Elias make a home in an uncivilized land. It appeared that she had some emotional territory to settle for her two men as well.

Walking as she mulled over this idea, Ruby moved closer to a fallen tree. Suddenly, her booted foot caught on a root. Dropping Buddy's hand she flailed and reached out a hand to steady herself against the nearest tree. It did no good and she fell forward.

As she went down, the whirr of a bullet passed her and exploded against the tree. Bark became shrapnel showering her, scraping her cheek as it flew past her. In a panic, she pulled Buddy down with her and wiggled across the ground to hide behind the tree. Peeking around it, she saw a figure clothed in a suit and a bowler hat, with greasy hair hanging below it, take aim again in her direction.

She wanted to whimper as she watched him approach the tree where they hid.

Curling herself around Buddy, she prayed out loud over them. After all, the man already knew where they hid. No need to be quiet. Not even thinking to yell her brother's name, she cried, "Jesus, help us."

The man was close enough now that she heard him laugh in response to her prayer. The laugh died quickly as the report from Onie's Henry rifle echoed in her ears. At the man's scream, she peered around the tree.

The man had dropped his gun. He held his left arm as he raced for his horse. Onie took aim but didn't fire. Instead, he jeered. "You'd better run. I should shoot you in the back. A man who would shoot a woman doesn't deserve more."

Once the man galloped away, Onie ran to her and helped her up. "You're bleeding! Did the bullet hit you?"

Putting a hand to her bloody cheek, she pulled it away and stared dumbly at her blood-coated fingers.

"It's just a scrape. Maybe from the flying bark or from my fall."

A movement over Onie's shoulder caught her attention. There, by the wagon, a man crept toward the baby.

Screaming, she raced to protect Letty. As she moved, Ruby yelled for the man to get away from the baby.

Onie bellowed, "You're a dead man if you touch my daughter." Sprinting for the baby, he passed Ruby who'd already started towards the wagon.

Before any of them could reach the infant, the small man grabbed her up and ran toward his horse. Desperate, Onie stopped running. Aiming, he shot the back of the man's knee. The kidnapper threw the infant as he dropped to the ground, immobilized by his wound.

"Letty!" Ruby screamed from behind her brother and watched with frightened eyes. Time seemed to slow as the baby sailed through the air like water thrown out of a pan.

The angry cry jerked her into action. Grabbing Buddy's hand, she rushed to the screaming baby. As she ran, Ruby threw a comment over her shoulder. "Better guard him so he doesn't shoot me in the back as I pass!" After all, what else could one expect from a man who would try to steal a baby?

Reaching Letty, Ruby collapsed onto the grass next to her. She had to since her legs no longer held her up after she saw the rock. It was jagged and large, sitting just to the right of where the baby landed. "Thank you, Lord! Thank you, thank you, Lord!"

Buddy looked at her oddly as she chanted her thanks. Evidently, he didn't understand how close Letty's head had come to the rock. The baby lay cocooned in long, springy grass. Ruby decided it had acted like a feather bed, cushioning her fall.

Gently running her hands over the baby's head and neck, she checked her over before feeling the wailing baby's flailing limbs. When Buddy held her small hand and started singing to her, Letty quieted somewhat.

Picking up the baby, Ruby headed back to the wagon. Once she reached the kidnapper, she gave him a hard kick above his wound. At the man's scream, she yelled at him, "I never thought I'd kick a man when he was down, but you deserve it! You almost killed this baby!"

"'tweren't my fault. This here wanted man's what almost did the baby in!" Then he let loose with a string of curses.

"Shut up," Onie bellowed, "if you want me to stop your bleeding. Won't be any hardship to let you spill out. Especially since your buddy tried to kill my sister."

Ruby's usual calm seemed to desert her. The panic of the last half-hour addled her mind, she decided, because she couldn't stifle the hysterical laugh that rose from deep inside of her. "And all for nothing, mister. My brother's not wanted. If you check with Sheriff Kidd, you'll find that out."

At the sound of horses approaching, Onie dropped the bandages and grabbed up his Henry rifle. Ruby rushed to the wagon, scrambling after Buddy into it.

"Lay down on the floor, Buddy. Hold the baby for me!" She hissed her command and watched as the boy obeyed, wrapping himself around Letty.

She crouched behind the tailgate and peered over it to watch the figures come near the camp. Relief caused her bones to become watery as she recognized her husband first and then Sheriff Kidd.

Kidd jumped down from his horse with a laugh. "Well now. This is a great sight. Wild Bob Meager shot in the leg!" He looked at Onie. "Can't tell you how often I've wanted to plug this bounty hunter. Man's a mean one."

The bounty hunter glared up at the sheriff. "You need to be arresting this man. He's wanted and he tried to kill me."

"That so? Looks to me like he hits what he aims for. Back of the leg, too. So you were running away from him? The boys at Tilly's saloon are gonna love this story when I get back to town." Sheriff Kidd's deep laughs echoed down to the river while Bob Meager glared at him.

Elias searched the camp and then rushed to the wagon when Ruby called to him. He reached up for her and pulled her into a crushing hug. Lowering his lips, he gave her a kiss that spoke more of relief than of passion.

Raising his head, he looked past her. "Kids in the wagon?"

At her nod, he lowered the back and caught Buddy as the boy catapulted into his father's arms. Left behind, Letty wailed and Ruby climbed into the vehicle to comfort her sweet girl.

Outside, she heard Kidd explain that Onie wasn't truly wanted. Foul language erupted from the wounded man while the sheriff continued with his belly laughs. Looking down at the baby as she removed her soiled diaper, Ruby whispered, "He really does hate that man, precious one." Then she softly admitted, "I'm not too fond of him, either. Still, I shouldn't have kicked him. I was a terrible example of forgiveness for Buddy."

Tears clung to the baby's lashes and she breathed raggedly from her crying. Ruby cradled her and reached for a towel to use as a swaddle. She spoke in a low, calm voice as she looked down at her cherub. "I hope your uncle found the bag with your extra things. With all the fuss, I didn't even get a fire started and haven't washed any of your clothes."

The baby sighed and rested against Ruby's chest. Ruby wished she could relax as easily. A question gnawed at her. *If that man was a bounty hunter, why did he try to take the baby?*

CHAPTER 9

"So they weren't sent by Tyson? Both of them were after Onie?"

Laying side by side under the canvas cover of the tent, Elias held his wife's hand and brought her fingers to his lips before answering her. "It had nothing to do with the Sauers. Just two men thinking to draw your brother out by using the baby as ransom."

"Why not surround him and, well, arrest him? And why shoot at me? None of this makes any sense." In the dark, he felt her confusion like it was a living thing hovering over top of them.

"Bob Meager didn't strike me as a very intelligent man. Mean, yes, but not intelligent." He released her hand and wrapped the arm around her. "Onie's known as a good shot, so Meager told me.

His partner shot at you to draw Onie out of camp. Then Meager slipped up on Letty. They planned to use her to force Onie into coming, unarmed, to a spot where they could easily get a hold of him."

Under his arm, he felt her exhale in a deep sigh. What she said next surprised him. "It's been such a rough night, and I still haven't learned to cook over a fire!" The whispered wail at the end brought a chuckle from him and she pulled away when she heard it.

"You think that's funny. Well, decide you're either eating burnt food or more of that tough beef you brought out tonight for us to suck on. I swear it took half an hour to get one piece soft enough to eat properly." Indignation had replaced the wail in her voice. He knew enough about women to stifle any more chortles. His wife was worn clear through and needed coddling, he suspected.

Leaning down, he gave her a tender kiss and moved his hand down to the middle of her back. He started rubbing gently as he spoke. "Tomorrow's another day. Sure enough, things didn't turn out as we thought. But, just think about it. You, Buddy, and Letty are safe. The ridiculous plan of those bounty hunters failed—I still can't wrap my head around how they thought that plan would work. It all happened when the sheriff had decided to ride out and speak to Onie about the telegrams he got."

At her sigh of contentment, he knew rubbing her back was the right thing to do and he pulled her tighter to him as his hand moved. The preacher's words about loving his wife came back to him. In that moment, he realized that the loving didn't have to involve words exchanged. It was found in the small acts.

Her sleepy voice asked a question then. "I was so busy with the children I never learned what the sheriff came out to say." She was relaxing enough to forget cooking over fires and strange bounty hunters. Good!

He continued his touch on her back but made it lighter as he sensed her almost ready to nod off. "Sheriff Kidd said the lawyer and the law in your hometown cleared Onie. He's going to spread the word. I gave him some money to have posters made, something he can mail to other lawmen letting them know the charge against one Onyx Hastings is false."

"Umm." She lay heavy against his shoulder as she made that sound. Laying on the ground under a canvas covering, he should be wishing for his bed back in Mills Bluff. Contentment filled him, instead. He had a helpmate and companion he could grow to love as he daily worked to show her love in return. He had two beautiful children sleeping nearby in the tent. Little ones to protect and nurture. Smiling, he fell asleep considering his blessings.

Cursed! That's how she felt this morning as she tried to start a fire and only produced smoke—and lots of it. The first breakfast she would cook for her husband might be more of that terrible beef jerky.

If they'd had a fire the evening before, she could have placed a pan of oatmeal in the coals for it to cook slowly during the night. The havoc caused by the two miscreants had even ruined her plans for an easy breakfast.

Here she sat, poking at a recalcitrant fire and wishing for home and her cookstove. *If wishes were*

horses, beggars would ride. No use wanting
something when life with her husband held much
more promise.

During the next two weeks, she reminded
herself often not to want the past when her future
with Elias was bright. With his help, she conquered
the knack of making fires and managed to cook
eatable meals—with a few blackened ones in the
very beginning. She'd cringed when she'd served
those early efforts, but Buddy had especially
enjoyed them. The child seemed to enjoy the taste
of burnt food and even asked for dark toast at the
only restaurant they'd eaten in during the past
couple weeks.

She'd quickly begun walking behind the wagon
on their trip. Her body ached less in the evening if
she ambled behind the wagon. It also allowed her
and Buddy to pick up kindling and firewood as they
followed behind. For the boy, each day became an
adventure and treasure hunt combined. He ran along
the trail with his eyes focused on the ground and
grass, collecting an amazing amount of sticks.

In far less than the two weeks she'd known him, Buddy had become the son of her heart. He clung to her neck each night as she settled him into his blankets and kissed her cheek before sighing a tired "Goodnight, ma'am." He wore himself out each day, but always kissed her goodnight. She would kiss his forehead as his eyes closed and tell him that she loved him. She'd easily grown to love him.

His father was a different story. Something about him kept her from being entirely comfortable in this marriage.

While she followed the wagon, she had time to think. To keep from missing her soft life at home, she considered what bothered her about Elias.

It certainly wasn't his treatment of her. He'd patiently taught her to cook over a fire and how to wash their clothes without a scrub board in the cold water of the river. Each night, he tenderly snuggled her close to him, though with two little ones in the tent their intimacy never went further.

In a way, she welcomed that. The lack of privacy gave her a chance to better discover what type of man her husband was. Just as Mrs.

Crenshaw had assured her, Ezra—she practiced thinking of him using this name—valued her and the children, protected and cared for them, and showed a strong sense of responsibility.

So, what bothered her about him? Why did she feel a barrier between them?

At night, before falling asleep, they laid under the blankets and talked. He asked questions about her home and life prior to marrying him. He wanted to know everything, it seemed, and peppered her with questions.

Last night, he'd held her close and, with confusion in his voice, had whispered, "Why weren't you already married? You're made to be a wife and mother. Are the men in your hometown all blind?"

"You must be the one who has weak eyes if you think I'm so perfect," she'd countered with a very soft laugh, not wanting to wake the children.

He'd pressed her, not letting her avoid the question. "I'm serious, you know. If I had greater faith, I might believe that the Lord saved you just for me."

She'd pulled back and looked up into his face. "Why not? Maybe marrying you was part of what the Lord had planned for me, like it says in Jeremiah twenty-nine."

He didn't say anything so she began to quote the verse. "For I know the thoughts I think toward you—" With a derisive snort from her husband, she stopped abruptly.

Remembering the moment a day later, she chastised herself for not pushing him. Instead, she curled away from him and said nothing more. This was the barrier between them. He refused to speak about himself or his life before their marriage. Well, he did tell her stories about Buddy's infancy and such, but never mentioned his wife in them. After the day when he'd explained about the Sauers, her husband was deaf to her questions about his past, and the wall between them became a wall around her heart that she determined he wouldn't penetrate.

At Buddy's excited, "Look!" she put a hand to the brim of her bonnet and searched the horizon. In the not too far distance, she saw the outline of wooden buildings against the flat Nebraska horizon. Onie and Elias—Ezra, she cautioned herself--had checked the map last evening, a nightly ritual, and discussed stopping in the small town of Bailey's Meadow.

Since the wagon veered from the trail and headed for the buildings, the two must have decided it was a town that might need a blacksmith or a livery. As lonely as it appeared, Bailey's Meadow did sit near a well-traveled trail just over the line from Kansas. Perhaps the men thought it might be a good place for a business because of that.

Elias—no, Ezra, she reminded herself--stopped the wagon and hopped down. He waited for her and then grinned. "Come sit with me in the wagon, Ruby mine. We'll view this place together." When she reached him, he swung her up and then climbed in. Tapping the leathers to the horses' backs, they were off again.

The unweathered appearance of the wooden buildings told Ruby that the town was young. Unpainted, raw wood comprised many of them.

One building was in the process of being painted. A young man holding a brush stood on a ladder and waved at them as their wagon rolled by. Buddy jumped up and down as he waved back, causing the painter to break out in a toothy grin. Another man fixed a sign to a one-story building. He turned, waving to them as well. At least, it seemed, the townspeople were friendly.

The wagon rolled to a stop in front of a single-story framed building. A sign lettered in cheery red proclaimed it Bailey's Mercantile. "It must be owned by the town's founder," her husband said with a chuckle. His tone sounded optimistic. "He's the one we need to chat with about the businesses in town. He'll know if there's a need for a blacksmith, I warrant."

Stepping inside, a short, red-haired man greeted them from behind a counter that stood parallel to the door. The store appeared to Ruby to be stocked with an amazing variety of goods, something she didn't expect in this small town. Bolts of fabric in tempting colors stood on a table near the front window. Books and toys were on a shelf beyond them. Near the back of the store, she spotted a table with produce and shelves with canned goods. Smart of the man to make his customers walk past the dry goods to reach the food they probably came to buy.

She walked to the shelf of toys, wanting to look over the rattles. While looking through the items, she heard her husband speak with the man who confirmed that Bailey's Meadow was indeed named after him.

"Blacksmith? Begorrah and that's just what we're needing!" He pumped Eli's hand in welcome. "I've several farmers living in the area. Homesteaders, you see. They've asked me to find someone to shoe the horses and fix their plows. The Lord above must have driven your team to my town!"

Ruby hid a smile at the man's exuberance. Still, she hoped they could stay here. Living out of a wagon had grown tiresome.

Choosing a set of wooden blocks rather than a rattle, she carried them to the counter. Mr. Bailey smiled her way before continuing his conversation with Elias.

"Need a freighter, too. But as I was sayin',
we've a livery of sorts. Just getting the business
started when he stepped on the nail. It not being
rusty, Cummings thought nought of it. Poor
muppet's foot went gammy. Were gone before
anyone could haul him over to the doc in Falls
City." With a hand over his heart, the man bowed
his head for a moment.

During this pause, Ruby threw a questioning
look at her husband. He smiled and nodded,
confirming he was interested in staying in this town.
She beamed in return. They might finally have a
home.

Raising his head again, Bailey moved around
the counter and to the door. With the wave of his
hand, he beckoned for Elias to follow him outside.
Pointing up the street, he motioned to a building at
the north edge of town. "See that one up there,
livery sign's on it so you won't be missing it.
Widow Cummings lives in the house behind it.
She's wanting to sell out. Plans to go to her sister's
family." With a happy slap to the younger man's
shoulders, which landed somewhere closer to the

bottom of his rib cage because of their height difference, Bailey headed back into the store.

"The children's blocks!" Ruby protested, as her husband took her arm to head up the street. "And shouldn't we tell Onie where we're headed."

He groaned and looked over his shoulder at the wagon. "I expect you're right. Go on back in and pay for the toys while I fill Onie in on the news."

When she left the store a second time, the family headed up the street in their wagon with Onie's horse tied to the back. Buddy sat behind the tailgate and spoke to it in a silly voice as they moved up the street. Letty giggled and cooed, letting everyone know that she enjoyed Buddy's silliness.

Peeking between the buildings, Ruby saw another street beyond the main one on each side of town. Only three streets to the whole town!

Doubt colored her voice when she spoke. "It's such a small place. Can you make a living here?"

Onie and Elias exchanged a tolerant look before her husband answered her. "Sweetheart, it's the farmers around us that will help us earn a living, not the people in town. Onie and I will freight goods into the area, too. That will help. We'll travel up to Plattsmouth and find out what men are charging to haul goods to the nearby towns."

Plattsmouth seemed very familiar to her. She searched her memory for the reason, scrunching her face in concentration.

"What has you frowning so?" Elias asked with his usual chuckle. "Is the sky about to fall?"

She shook her head at his silliness. "I'm trying to remember when I've heard of Plattsmouth. I can't place it, but I know I should."

With his gloved hand, he chucked her under the chin. "Good thing I remember since that's where your crates are waiting for you." Lifting her into the wagon, he started the team.

It was a short journey up the street to the livery. Though small, it did have double doors to allow wagons easy access to the building. Two small trees had been planted on either side of the double doors. At the sight of them, she snapped her fingers.

Her husband looked at her strangely so she smiled to reassure him. "That's what's missing. Trees. The town is so barren." They'd passed a small stand of trees, ash she thought, not far from the town. If they stayed here, she and Buddy would dig up saplings and plant them around the livery.

Both doors were thrown open and a nicely-garbed woman sat primly on a straight back chair, knitting. She raised a careworn face and frowned. "You'll need to see to your beasts yourself. Fifty cents a night for each animal." Without waiting for a response, her hands busily started working the yarn.

Having removed his leather gloves, her husband helped her out of the wagon. Ruby whispered near his ear, "Poor lady. I can see in her face how much she hates this place."

After being sure she was standing securely on the ground, he ran a finger over her cheek. "Always the nurturer. Perhaps the Lord brought us here to help her. One of those plans of His you yammer about."

She sniffed indignantly but was secretly pleased. He had listened to her about the Lord's leading!

She turned to lift Letty out of her basket. When she straightened up, she realized he'd left her.

Hustling to catch up with her husband's long stride, she moved to stand by his side as he introduced them. "Ezra King, ma'am, and my wife Ruby. Are you Mrs. Cummings?"

Not answering, the woman took Eli's measure and stopped to stare at his capable, work-worn hands. "Bet you're wanting to run the livery. Something in me said the Lord would be answering my prayer today."

Rising from the chair, she placed the knitting on the seat and inclined her head toward the interior of the place. "Come on in and see Mr. Cummings' set up." The woman's eyes and face hardened then and she spoke coldly as she stared up at Elias. "Mind you, I'm not looking to take on a partner, Mr. King. It's a buyer I'm dealing with or I'm not dealing at all."

With no trace of his usual jocularity, he gave her an abrupt nod. "I was a business owner back east and my own man. Don't expect I'd want to share my place with anyone."

The widow seemed to brighten at his words. She hustled them into the livery with Onie and Buddy following behind them. The building had a loft and four stalls, fewer than any Ruby had seen in a business of this sort. She kept quiet, not wanting to intrude by asking why Mr. Cummings had made the place this small. Harnesses hung neatly on the walls and everything seemed orderly. The two occupied stalls had been mucked and the smell of new hay floated down from the loft.

Elias must have noticed the few stalls. He rubbed a hand over his jaw before asking, "Never seen a livery with only four stalls. Not much call to rent horses hereabouts?"

Mrs. Cummings turned away from the tack she'd been straightening and frowned. "It's expensive to have the lumber brought out. Just try to build this place for the price I'm asking out of it!" With a huff, she moved to the mucking tools and scooped debris from behind one of the horses. She immediately took the bucket outside through a back door. Ruby followed and watched her empty it into a cart.

When she looked over her shoulder, Onie and Elias had their heads close together, whispering and pointing to spots in the room. Jostling a fussy Letty, she faced the other woman. "I understand you plan to sell the house as well. May I see it, please?"

With a nod, the older woman led her to the wood-framed house. While the livery itself wasn't painted, the house boasted a coat of slate-blue. Small saplings had been planted on both sides of the house. Small rose bushes stood to each side of the white porch steps. The woman obviously loved her home.

"The color is lovely. I'd expect it to be white, but this color is one that has become very popular in my hometown in Massachusetts."

The widow beamed. "I had my sister send it out. I do like pretty things." Then her expression abruptly changed. "I'd hoped it would help me forget this horrible, barren prairie. No trees, nothing green and lovely."

Unable to stop herself, Ruby looked beyond the home to the horizon. Though the summer heat had begun to turn the grass brown in spots, wildflowers and a sea of waving green met her eyes. She saw freedom and beauty. How this poor woman must hate this place if she couldn't see that.

While she'd been staring at the prairie, Mrs. Cummings had moved to stand by the home's front door. "Please, come on up and we'll go inside." She held her hand out in invitation before opening the screen door. Ruby followed and was transported back East.

Though small, the home still had a foyer and she could imagine her mother's coat tree sitting against one of the walls. The spot would be perfect for it. An open staircase stood opposite the front door, made of oak if her guess was correct. To the right, pocket doors stood shut. To the left of the stairs was a hallway that led deeper into the house. An open archway to the left of the room allowed her to glimpse a dining room table and a door that led off of that room, probably to the kitchen.

Her hostess slid back the pocket doors and led her into a parlor. The red damask sofa and matching armchairs spoke of the woman's privileged background. The rich brocade curtains and doilies contrasted with her actions moments before of shoveling horse manure. The room conveyed a longing, almost a homesick feeling and Ruby had to swallow the lump that had formed in her throat to be able to speak.

Working to sound complimentary and yet mundane, Ruby forced her mind to form the questions she needed to ask. "How elegant, Mrs. Cummings. You have lovely taste. Will you be taking the furniture with you?"

With a sad shake of her head, Mrs. Cummings wrapped her arms around her middle. "No, I can't see freighting it to the train and then paying to ship it. I'm staying with my sister's family, you see. Her things are so much nicer than mine. She married well." The woman looked around her elegant parlor and snorted in derision. Much of the pity Ruby had felt vanished with the woman's condescension, allowing her to focus more easily on the business at hand.

"Please, take me into your kitchen."

The woman led her out the pocket doors and then turned to close them, guarding her sanctum, it seemed. They walked through the open archway into the dining room. As Ruby had suspected, the door in the far wall of that room led into the kitchen. When she stepped through it, the stove immediately caught her eye. It was identical to the one she'd been missing for these weeks on the trail. Unable to resist, she moved to it and ran her hand over the warm metal in what was almost a caress.

Mrs. Cummings cleared her throat and Ruby caught the woman's odd look at her action. She didn't care. This room powerfully drew something in her. The warm loaf of bread on the table and the neatly lined dishes in the door-less cupboards whispered "home" to her.

"I will be leaving everything here, of course. I even have some of the garden truck already canned and in the pantry. She pointed to a door to the right of the stove.

"How wonderful." She could tell that the woman didn't treasure this kitchen, didn't like to be in the room. Still, she imagined Mrs. Cummings would be a competent cook, as she seemed to be careful about everything she did. Surely, her preserved foods would be safe to eat.

"Now, may I see the upstairs?"

As the woman led her back through the dining room, she mentioned Letty. "You have a very clean child. That does say something about you, even if you are wearing one of those horrid shortened skirts. Oh, the filthy little urchins I see coming in from the farms around here. You would not believe the way those *people* choose to live." Mrs. Cummings' intonation when she said the word indicated that she considered them to be something less than human. No wonder the woman would sell for less than the cost they put into the house just to escape the area. Did she have any friends in town, Ruby wondered?

At the top of the stairs, three doors faced the hallway, one on the right and two on the left. Opening the single door to the right, the older woman stepped into the room and Ruby followed her. Obviously the master bedroom, the cherry wood suite gleamed, even though little light penetrated the room. The windows faced east so light must flood the room in the morning. At this time of day, less of it filtered in through the windows. Still, she could see well enough to appreciate the size of the room and the quality of the furniture. Here again, Ruby realized that Mrs. Cummings demanded the best. What had her husband's life been like with this woman?

"The other rooms aren't furnished. I didn't see the need since my sister would never come to visit us and no one else would be welcomed." The woman's tone was flat. Ruby didn't prod her to explain.

"You never had children?" She kissed Letty's forehead as she asked the question. The patient baby patted her cheek. Playful, Ruby captured the little hand with her lips and pretended to eat it. Giggles poured from the rosebud mouth.

"Certainly not!" Mrs. Cummings lost her flat tone, appalled at Ruby's question. She eyed the antics between woman and baby with antipathy.

"Not every woman is born to be a mother, I suppose." Moving around the woman, she exited the room. While she loved the house, Ruby knew she would need to make changes to erase the cold atmosphere stamped on it by its owner.

Not bothering to look in the unfurnished rooms, Ruby descended the stairs and went out the door. Outside, she raised her face to the summer sun and smiled at the feeling of warmth on her face.

"Ruby!" Elias loudly called her name, a note of desperation in his voice.

"At the house."

He rushed around the corner of the livery and clasped her tightly against him. "You were gone and I was sure something must have happened. It was like the day Mary drowned." Her upbeat husband had never betrayed a hint of worry before this. She realized now that the trauma of a few months past did haunt him still, even if he'd kept it carefully hidden.

"The business is your concern. Mine is the house, so I took a tour of it. Well, a tour of everything except the cellar." She considered that now, but dismissed it as being unimportant. "I like what I see and think we'd be happy here. That is, if you decide to purchase it."

"I never wanted to run a livery. I grew up helping in one since my father had his smithy business joined with a livery." She thought he seemed tired as he sighed and loosened his hug, leaving just one arm around her shoulders. "There's plenty of room to build a smithy. It'll do for us."

He might simply be settling. She felt like a bird coming back to its nest. Home!

The delay overwhelmed her.

When Tyson lost Kline's trail, she'd become anxious. Because of that, she'd had to start wearing a wig. The bald spots showed where she'd pulled out her hair. Not only had Kline stolen her boy, but now she had ruined her beautiful hair.

That ridiculous Scotts marshal hadn't helped either. Imagine an outsider coming in to ask about the deaths. He even dared interrogate her.

As if Mary deserved justice, the tart. The only good thing she'd done in life was to birth little Franz for her.

It all had changed that day. Finally, Tyson knew where they'd gone. She'd listened at the door and heard the name—Bailey's Meadow, Nebraska.

This time, she would go with Tyson. No one in the family would stop her.

CHAPTER 10

They lived out of the wagon for another two days, camping out beyond the house and sleeping in the tent. Mrs. Cummings and Eli had reached an agreement about the sale of the property, but the woman needed the extra days to pack, she'd said, and thoroughly clean the house.

Ruby remembered the conversation. "It seems fine to us, ma'am," she'd told the woman, not wanting her to fuss over the house.

Even though she was much shorter than Ruby, the woman managed to look down her nose as she bristled at Ruby's words. "Not clean it? My dear, one never leaves a home that way." At her condescension, Ruby abandoned the conversation and left the woman to do what she wanted.

Today, Mrs. Cummings would leave. Dread weighed on Ruby's shoulders at the thought. It meant the men would go as well.

As she watched, her husband helped the widow onto the seat of their wagon. He'd emptied his smithy tools into a stall and moved their baggage to the house so there would be room to haul crates back from the train depot. Onie would drive the livery's wagon to freight back any orders for the mercantile that might be waiting there.

The night before, after the little ones were asleep, she and her husband lay awake while he whispered his plans. "I'll find out what others are charging to freight goods. Bailey told me what he's willing to pay. I agreed to it for now, but told him I would be checking on the going rates for future loads."

While she willed herself to relax, nonetheless her shoulders still stiffened. "I hate being left here." When he began to protest, she reached out and patted the arm that lay nearest her. "I know. The children and I are added weight for the horses to pull. But, well—" Embarrassed, she paused and then decided to continue. "I've grown very fond of you. I'll miss you."

Wrapping her in his arms, he pulled her forward and kissed her softly. The touch was like velvet pulled across her lips. Then he raised his head. "It's nice to know you aren't ready to get rid of me. You know, I wanted one night in that big bedroom before I left." He gave a quiet chuckle. "I couldn't figure out how to make that happen when Mrs. Cummings was still in it."

Now, as he prepared to leave, Elias embraced Buddy and ruffled the boy's curls. When his father lowered him to the ground, Buddy ran back to the porch. Minutes before, Ruby gave him the blocks she purchased their first day in Bailey's Meadow. Letty lay on her stomach on top of a light quilt, wiggling her limbs and staring at the block towers Buddy built for her. So far, she hadn't been able to reach one to chew. Before the day was over, Ruby suspected the baby would manage to do that.

Taking her eyes away from her husband, she glimpsed Onie pick up the baby and kiss her forehead. The action revealed that he found his daughter as irresistible as the rest of the family did. Hopefully, he'd settle nearby them so she wouldn't lose contact with the girl she secretly thought of as her own.

Looking her way, her brother set the baby back on her quilt. "Ruby, you remember what I taught you about using the colt. Don't forget to shoot high since your aim is off." Then he clomped down the porch steps and stopped at her side. Fishing in his pocket, he pulled out a small gun. "Keep this derringer in your apron pocket." She took it from him and tucked it in the apron, something she'd started wearing again that morning.

A hand to her arm brought her attention back to her husband. He gently pulled her through the back door of the livery stable, empty now of horses— except for her brother's gelding--since the teams were harnessed for the trip. Her husband had placed a sign out front, letting any customers know that they would need to feed and care for their horses and then pay at the house. Secretly, Ruby prayed no one would come while he was away.

In the darkness of the livery, she squinted to make out her husband's expression. "Did you need to speak with me in private?"

He shook his head silently. With a hand on either side of her face, he warmly kissed her. "I needed to say goodbye properly is all." Then he held her close to him. She thought she heard him whisper, "My heart," but couldn't imagine such sentiment from this man who maintained an emotional barrier.

Stepping away from her, he said, "Two nights," and then he strode purposefully outside. Climbing the wagon, he waved to Buddy who jumped up and down on the porch as he waved both hands in return. With a hand to shade her eyes, she watched her protectors roll away.

Concealing her fear, she walked to the porch and smiled at the children. Buddy placed the last block on top of the tower and then toppled it with one swipe of his hand. The baby startled and puckered her lip before the boy kneeled by her and rolled her onto her back. Tickling her tummy he said, "Don't cry, Letty. It's fun not scary." At his laugh and tickles, she chortled, and Ruby couldn't help but laugh with them.

Wanting clean bedding for the night, she heated water on the stove—her own stove—and stripped the large bed. The children would sleep with her while Elias was away. Thank the Lord for their comforting presence.

The day and night passed slowly, even with all the work she had to do in unpacking and ironing clothes and the now clean sheets. She was thankful that, when the new day dawned, it was Sunday. Through Mr. Bailey, she'd learned that there would be a potluck after church. Not only would she and the children be able to worship, but they would have companionship afterward.

After feeding Buddy his oatmeal and bathing Letty, she dressed them both in the best she had for them. When money was available, she'd get fabrics and sew church outfits for each. She suspected that there would be others dressed humbly at the church. This was the prairie, after all, and many were struggling to establish themselves and survive. A dress by Worth would hardly be their first concern. And that was good since she didn't own one.

Letty would need diapers and a bottle while they were absent from home. At first, Ruby feared she would have to show up at the church with a carpetbag. How odd that would look!

She searched the pantry and found nothing to use. When she looked in the linen closet, tucked under the stairs, she found a canvas rucksack and seized it like she'd discovered the prize in a treasure hunt. Stuffing the necessary items, along with Letty's rattle, into the bag, she stopped to examine her children again.

Her children! She thought of both that way, even if she hadn't birthed them. Just like her precious Emmie, they were trusted to her to raise and she was thankful for that.

Putting the rucksack on Buddy's back, he grinned at her. "Well, you look proud to help," she teased as she put a hand tenderly on his cheek. The boy nodded, his brown curls flopping. She would need to cut his hair soon, she thought absently. Turning away from him, she picked up Letty with one arm and a large towel tied around two dozen dinner rolls. Her contribution to the potluck that she'd baked early this morning when she woke early and couldn't get back to sleep.

Bailey's Meadow's only church was beyond the mercantile and one street behind it. Actually, on the only street behind it. The summer weather had been dry, allowing her to walk on the side of the dirt road. Twice, she had to tell Buddy not to kick the dirt. The boy gloried in watching the dust fly up into the air and his pants and boots showed traces of his activity. She'd need to brush him off before they entered the church building.

After he kicked the dirt the first time, Letty chortled. This made him do it again, of course. He loved to entertain the baby.

"Buddy Kline, if you do not stop that you will be sitting with me during the potluck. Wouldn't you rather be able to play?" Her stern voice left him in no doubt of her seriousness. Though it had been rare, she'd disciplined him before and he knew she would follow through with any punishment she promised.

Ducking his head, he contritely mumbled, "Yes, Mama."

Lightning shot through her at the name. She had the urge to drop the food she carried and hug her son. He'd said mama. It was the first time he used that name.

"Thank you, Buddy. I'm proud you're listening to me." When he looked up at her words, she smiled. "And I love that you called me your mama. That's what I am."

Buddy moved to her and hugged her around the waist. "I love you, Mama."

She didn't have a free arm or hand. The best she could do was awkwardly stoop and kiss his curly head and that was what she did. Then, with Buddy walking by her side, they finished the trip to the church.

The small, wood-framed building had been painted white. A cross stood on the peak of the church in place of a belfry. Two steps led into its single room. Sitting on an ocean of grass, the church building was surrounded by wagons, buggies, and groups of visiting congregants. With no bell, she wondered how they would know to go in for service. What called them to worship?

Tables to one side groaned with pans and plates of food. Ruby walked to one and a prosperously dressed woman with just a hint of grey in her dark hair met her there. "Good morning, what have you there?" Her voice was genial and her smile welcoming.

Returning the smile, Ruby held out the offering. "Dinner rolls. I wrapped them in towels to keep them warm." After saying that, pink flared in Ruby's cheeks. It didn't matter why they were wrapped in the towels. What a silly thing to say!

Reassuringly, the woman crooned, "What a good idea. And it protects them from the flies. The filthy things are terrible here on the prairie. But, of course, you've realized that by now. Screens on the windows are a saving grace during the summer."

When the woman stopped speaking, she suddenly put a hand to her mouth. "How silly of me. I never introduced myself. I'm Edna Bailey." This surprised Ruby. She'd expected Mrs. Bailey to be Irish, like her husband. Instead, this woman spoke with what seemed to be a refined southern accent. Perhaps, someday, Ruby would hear the story behind their marriage. She was sure it would be an interesting tale.

"I'm pleased to make your acquaintance, Mrs. Bailey. If you haven't already realized it, my husband is the one who purchased Mrs. Cummings' property. I'm Ruby King."

The two women chatted for a few more minutes, but a call from the doorway of the church stopped them. While Mrs. Bailey hurried away, Ruby held back and allowed the others to enter first.

En masse, people flowed into the stuffy building, picking up paper fans from a wooden chair just inside the doorway. On one side of each fan was printed an advertisement for Bailey's Mercantile and on the other was a black and white etching of Christ praying in the garden. A wooden handle, rather like a tongue depressor used by a doctor, had been attached to each fan.

One aisle ran up the center of the church. On each side of it stood short pews, only long enough to seat three adults comfortably. Already, pews were crammed with four adults or two adults with many children. As small as the town was, she marveled at the number of people who packed into the church. Mr. Bailey had been truthful when he'd told them that many farmers lived close to the town.

Mrs. Bailey gestured for Ruby to join her in a pew at the front of the church. Appreciating the offer, even if she'd rather hide in a back corner, she passed dozens of eyes and made her way to the woman. Smiling her thanks, she joined the now seated older woman and settled Letty on her lap. Buddy sat between the two adults until Mr. Bailey joined them.

"May I hold you," Mrs. Bailey asked the boy. His expression suddenly shy, the boy pulled away from her.

Forcing herself not to be embarrassed by her son's refusal, Ruby spoke up quickly. "The baby is growing heavy in my arms. Would you be willing to hold her instead? Buddy can sit on my lap while you do that."

Mrs. Bailey held out eager arms for the baby. Always compliant, Letty allowed the stranger to take her and Buddy settled quickly onto his mama's lap for their first church service together.

The familiar hymns helped Ruby feel at home. After the first hymn, Reverend Borgeson welcomed her publicly and asked her to stand for an introduction to the congregation. For his sermon, the young pastor read from the twenty-third Psalm and spoke about allowing the Lord to direct in each person's life. He compared his congregation to a herd of cows. While it might have been humorous on one level, Ruby appreciated that the man wanted to connect the lesson with what his parishioners experienced daily.

Once the final prayer had been spoken, the congregation surprised Ruby by suddenly loudly singing the doxology. She looked around and realized it must be a part of their weekly worship. No one's face showed the surprise she felt at hearing a song after the final prayer. Next week, she'd know to expect it and would join in.

Mrs. Baily held the sleeping baby. Reluctantly, the woman handed the child to Ruby. "She's such a dear! I'd go on holding her, but I'm expected to help outside."

Standing up, the woman smoothed out the wrinkles in her dress. Before she left, she invited Ruby to join her. "You'll see my bright red and white checked cloth. When you get your food, sit there. We'll be able to chat as we eat."

Relieved to have a companion during lunch, Ruby thanked her. Mrs. Bailey hurried away, but Ruby didn't stand alone for long. Several women introduced themselves and chatted briefly with her. Before long, Buddy had made a friend and the two boys scampered outside to join a game of tag.

Bless Edna Bailey, she'd brought extra plates for guests—something Ruby had forgotten to bring with her and, shamefaced, had confessed to the woman. With an angelic giggle, the woman produced extra plates and explained that it often happened that someone needed one of her "emergency" plates and cutlery. "People forget it's potluck Sunday, you know," she explained in a comforting tone. "Now, don't think another thing about it. Just join the line and fill that plate."

Once she and Buddy had food, they found Mr. Bailey on the red checked cloth and began to sample the foods. Letty fussed and Ruby gave her a bit of dinner roll to suck on. It had pleased her to see that the rolls were almost gone. Every woman loved to see what she brought eaten first at a potluck.

Soon Mrs. Bailey joined them. While Ruby finished eating, the other woman gave Letty her bottle. "It's been so long since I've cared for a child. Our daughters are grown and live in the East. Married, so they didn't join us out here." Ruby thought that explained the woman's tender care of Letty. She probably had grandchildren and missed them.

While they chatted, Buddy had left to play with his new friend again. Keeping an eye on her son, she still managed to carry on a conversation until she saw the man.

To the edge of the mercantile, a man with an oddly curved scar on his right cheek watched her son. She was sure of it. When Buddy moved farther away from the back of the mercantile, the man moved as well. Ruby watched his eyes dart in whatever direction Buddy went. When Buddy and his friend would have entered the alley between two buildings, she called urgently to him.

Her usually cheerful boy sullenly marched to her. "Sit on the blanket with me," she ordered.

"Mama, I wasn't being bad. You said if I was good, I wouldn't have to sit." His voice held a wailing note to it. He sounded tired and it gave her an excuse.

"I can hear in your voice that you need a nap." Before she rose, Ruby pointed to the man and asked the woman she now was familiar with, "Edna, do you know that man?"

The woman squinted against the sun and eyed him. "No, he's a stranger. And a rough-looking one, too." So she also picked up on the menace he gave off.

Regardless of the warm day, a shiver ran down Ruby's back. "Buddy's tired, and truth to tell, that man is watching him intently. Mr. Bailey," she turned her focus to the man who reclined at the edge of the cloth, "would you escort us home?"

That night, she couldn't relax. Letty had fretted and even Buddy's antics didn't cheer her. Ruby decided the baby must have sensed her fear and worked to put the stranger out of her mind as she held the baby. A rocking chair would have been a help in soothing the baby. The rocker belonging to Ruby's grandmother was part of the furniture she shipped, and she looked forward to being able to use it again.

Buddy, on the other hand, seemed oblivious to the tension in his new mother. He smiled up at her when she tucked him under the sheet. His new friend, he told her, would see him again next Sunday.

"What's your friend's name?" She smoothed the curls back from his forehead and kissed him.

Buddy's face scrunched into a frown. His thin shoulders shrugged. "I don't know. I think I forgot."

Oh to be a child again. Having fun and being with a playmate was more important than knowing a name. "It doesn't matter. You can ask him at church next week."

He'd fallen asleep quickly and Ruby left the room. She puttered around in her kitchen, rearranging cupboards in a way that made sense to her. Afterward, she sorted linens in the closet under the stairs. Mrs. Cummings had an unbelievable number of bath towels. What couple needed more than two or three bath towels? Did the woman bathe daily?

After the parlor clock chimed the midnight hour, Ruby gave up on the day. While she felt too edgy to sleep, she decided to lay down anyhow. Perhaps she would relax enough to sleep and could finally put the memories out of her mind of the stranger's odd expression as he watched Buddy.

As her fingers went to the buttons on her dress, a sound caught her attention. Below, a board creaked. She knew that board. It was the first floorboard after leaving the kitchen to enter the dining room. Lifting the oil lamp in one hand, she grabbed up her pistol with the other.

In the hallway, she set the lamp in the corner nearest the top of the stairs. Going to a dark corner at the other end of the hall, she set the pistol on the floor and hurried to retrieve the shotgun. Exiting the bedroom, she shut the door and moved to hunker down behind a heavy armchair Mrs. Cummings had placed—one that was at the dark end of the hallway.

There she listened to soft footfalls on the staircase. If the treads were carpeted, she wouldn't have been able to hear them so she was glad that the previous owner hadn't added that. Even as terror gripped her, she wondered if she would be able to shoot the intruder. If she did shoot, would she hit him? Her aim was far from accurate.

Why didn't Bailey's Meadow have a sheriff? When Elias returned, she would urge him to speak to Mr. Bailey about one.

As the figure passed the lamp, she recognized the stranger. He carried a drawn pistol and stepped lightly, almost walking on his tiptoes. The click when she drew back the hammer on the colt stopped him.

Whirling, he fired blindly. She had taken time to aim and squeezed off her first shot with care. Even aiming, she hit him in the thigh rather than the shoulder as she'd tried to do. As the bullet slammed into him, she took advantage of the moment to send another projectile his way. This time, he dropped with a cry of pain.

Picking up the shotgun, she reached the downed man in a few steps. Taking care to watch if he reached for his dropped pistol, she'd taken those few steps slowly. At his side, Ruby kicked his gun away and nudged his body with the barrel of her shotgun.

Eyes opened and stared up at her. "He's not even your son, Mrs. Kline. Let him go, so my boss don't kill you and that little baby, too."

A cry from the bedroom startled her. As she turned in response, the wounded man suddenly lifted himself and shoved her against the wall. With blood pouring from his wounds, where had he found the strength to act?

Slamming hard against the wall, Ruby saw flashes of light from the pain at the back of her head. She shook it quickly and gripped the shotgun, afraid the intruder would attack her.

The man was intent on making his way to the stairs, dragging his wounded leg as he went. A set of feet already pounded down the stairs. Who else had been up here? While she'd bent over the man, his partner must have made his way up the stairs. How was that possible?

Not bothering to grab the lamp, she flew into the bedroom, screaming Buddy's name. Letty's wails joined her screams. Buddy, if he lay in the bed, was silent.

Below, a door slammed shut. Running to the window, Ruby pushed on the screen and leaned out of it as she called for Buddy. His plaintive, "Mama, hel—" was cut off abruptly as a tinkle of high-pitched feminine laughter drifted on the breeze.

CHAPTER 11

Eli pushed the team until he realized they would have to make camp for the night. Even though he'd promised to be home in two days, Ruby's crates weighed heavily on the teams as well as the wagon axels. As it was, he'd been forced to buy two extra horses to create the team of four needed to pull the heaviest load.

Pulling the wagons to the edge of the trail, the two men set up camp. Now, sitting with his brother-in-law in front of the small fire they'd started to cook a rabbit, he pondered the question of names. "Onie, you glad to be using your real name again?"

The other man startled. Evidently, he had been lost in his thoughts, Eli guessed. Rubbing his jaw in embarrassment, he wished now he'd kept quiet.

Onie stared rather than answering, adding to his discomfort.

Finally, when Onie spoke, his voice conveyed his befuddlement. In the dim light of the fire, Eli could just see the man's raised eyebrows. "What bee you got in your bonnet? I've been using my real name for the last month."

Running both hands down his face, Elias groaned. "There's no wanted poster on me, but I changed my name anyhow. If I stay in Bailey's Meadow, I'm stuck being called Ezra King. I'd kinda like people to know me by the right name."

"That's all that's bothering you?" Onie roared with laughter.

Starting to rise, Elias decided to get his bedroll set up under the wagon. It was well after midnight by now. A firm grip on his arm pulled him down again.

Onie had contrived a serious expression as he held up a hand to stop Eli from speaking. "Okay, I get it. But, you're stuck in that town now. Did you see my sister's face as she walks through the house? You won't tear her away from it."

Smiling, Elias nodded. "It's the best part. She's pleased, even if the livery's small and there's no smithy yet for me. Glad to give my family a home." He heard the satisfaction in his voice but didn't mind. His wife and son, and now Letty, were essential to his very being. With difficulty, he acknowledged to himself that Ruby possessed a part of him unclaimed by any other. Somehow in his mind, he couldn't acknowledge that and let their closeness grow until he could openly be Elias Kline again.

Onie's advice suddenly seemed essential to Elias' future. And he would once again be Elias. Somehow!

"So, what do you think I should do? About the name thing, I mean."

A moment of silence hung between them before Onie spoke. "Well, Mr. Bailey seems like a decent sort. Go to him and explain the situation. You can even show him the telegram that Marshal Ferguson sent you in Plattsmouth. Good news that he'll be making an arrest in Mills Bluff soon."

Any response Elias might have made was halted by the sound of horses. Onie gripped his Henry while Elias readied his shotgun for trouble. Both men kicked dirt over the fire, not wanting to make themselves any easier of targets.

By now, they could tell the horses were headed north on the trail, away from Bailey's Meadow. "Must be driven by a fool," Onie snorted, "traveling that fast through these ruts and at night."

It was a fact, no doubt about it. Though no response was needed for that statement, Elias relaxed his guard a bit and a comment slipped out. "Doesn't seem like a group of marauders. That's for sure."

A buggy came into view, it's lighter weight bouncing along a trail meant for heavier wagons. Since the men had camped to the right of the trail, Elias barely made out the silhouette of a woman driving the vehicle. What he did see was a familiar curly head.

"Buddy!"

At his loud exhalation of the name, the boy started calling for him. "Help, Daddy! Dad—" The words were cut off as the woman whipped the pair of dark horses into even greater speed. The crack of the leather on their backs echoed in Elias' ears.

Shouting Buddy's name, he watched the buggy fly down the trail. Buddy's face poked out the side to catch a last view of his father and it tore a roar of pain from Elias.

The typically self-centered Onie sprang into action, ready with an idea. "Good thing that new pair of horses you bought can be ridden." Sprinting toward the ground tied horses, he removed the tether and used the dark mane, swinging himself up on the large Belgian's back. Gripping the barrel chest of the horse with his short legs, Onie took off at a gallop without bothering to watch Elias mount.

Swinging his large frame onto the other Belgian, Elias meant to put heels to its side and head after Onie. The rapid hoofbeats coming from the south stopped him.

A female Valkrie from German tales his father had told, hair streaming behind her as the woman rode by him. When she passed, he saw a baby tied to her back. The woman, the gelding, the baby—all were familiar and dear to him. Urging his mount, he joined the pursuit.

The female avenger looked over her shoulder at the sound of his horse. Amazement and then relief chased across her features. She cried his name with delight but didn't slow her pace.

The heavier Belgian struggled to keep up with the sleek gelding, even though that animal already had run for miles. Because of that, Elias followed rather than raced alongside her, making any discussion impossible. The how and the who would need to wait until the buggy was stopped.

A loud crack sounded. Gunfire?

By the tiniest hint of dawn, he made out the shape of the buggy. It tipped to one side, letting him know she'd broken an axel or the wheel. That had caused the loud crack.

Coming on the scene, Ruby vaulted with amazing ease from the bare back of the gelding. A truly stupendous act, considering the baby she carried on her back.

With the bark of her name and an upheld hand, Onie stopped her from approaching her son. Still on the back of the Belgian, Elias looked down on the scene. The woman held a small pistol to his son's temple.

Easing off the horse, Elias held up his hands as he moved to stand by Onie. "Don't recall who you are, ma'am. I know we've met."

A hysterical laugh bubbled up out of the woman's chest. "No one ever does remember me. It doesn't matter since all you need to know is that I'm Little Franz's mother." The woman squeezed Buddy as she said that, causing him to cry out.

At Ruby's sound of protest, Elias waved a hand behind him. She needed to stay quiet while he dealt with this strange woman.

At the sound of her voice, Buddy yelled, "I want Mama." His sobbing punctuated the cry.

"I'm here, baby." The woman crooned to him even as the little boy pushed against her and struggled to escape.

Keeping his voice neutral as he spoke, Elias reasoned with the kidnapper. "Ma'am, I was there at my son's birth. *You* are definitely not his mama." Would logic reach this woman's mind?

A growl erupted from her throat. "He's meant to be mine. Mary Schmidt was just a vessel. A handmaiden like Haggar in the Bible."

The biblical reference suddenly reminded Elias of when he'd seen this woman. "You're Franz Sauer's wife, aren't you?"

She didn't answer that question. Ranting, she poured out her pain and her plot.

"All would have been fine without that nosy Marshal Ferguson. I'd taken care of Mary. She could have lived if she agreed to give him to me." She stared at Elias with her strangely wide-set eyes. "You can see that she had to die for refusing to give him to me." A sob broke off her words.

"Mrs. Sauer, I don't see that at all. Did your husband know what you did?" Working hard to keep the anger and disgust out of his voice, Elias pushed her to speak about Franz. Had his wife killed him?

Dropping the small pistol to the ground, Mrs. Sauer hugged Buddy to her breast. "He couldn't see that the Lord wanted me to have Little Franz. I heard the voice tell me to kill her, but he wouldn't believe me. Said he would take me far away from my darling Little Franz. I had to shoot him with this." She raised her hand and screeched as she gazed at her empty hand.

Three adults rushed her. Onie and Elias each grabbed a demonically strong arm while Ruby ripped her sobbing son from the woman's embrace.

Watching Ruby curl her body around his son, Elias ached to be part of their hug. Emotion and relief toppled his barriers as he heard himself say, "Ruby, I love you!"

It was hard to tell which person was more surprised by his words. Onie gave him a strange look and then shook his head. "You have no sense of timing."

Ruby's mouth gaped and she stared. Even in shock, her arms still cradled Buddy close to her. Closing her mouth, she narrowed her eyes. "Tell me again when it's just the two of us, Ezra King." The words came out sounding like a dare.

"Elias Kline will take that challenge, woman." His chuckle dispersed the last of the fear. Whether the people of Mills Bluff would ever accept that this woman was the murderer and not him didn't matter. He wouldn't return there.

Ezra King was no more. Elias Kline now lived in Bailey's Meadow.

The next few hours were awkward. Without rope to restrain her, Elias rode with a struggling Mrs. Sauer laid across his lap. He balanced with difficulty on the bare back of the horse, keeping a hand pressed to the center of the woman's back.

Onie led the lathered horses who'd been hitched to the buggy. With its broken wheel, the buggy had been left behind. Perhaps later in the day, one of them could come out to fix it and then retrieve it.

When they reached the heavily-laden wagons, Elias sighed with relief to be rid of the woman. Onie retrieved the rope and bound her. To shut her up, he stuffed a white handkerchief in her mouth before laying her between bundles and crates in the back of his wagon.

It was an odd-looking caravan that arrived in Bailey's Meadow at dawn, Elias thought. Both wagons had horses tied to the tailgate. He wondered who owned the horses hitched to the buggy. He'd have Onie ask around in Plattsmouth next time he visited to freight goods. Elias, himself, wouldn't go. He didn't plan to leave his family for a good long time.

On the ride back, Buddy cuddled between his parents with Letty napping at Ruby's feet on a blanket. Occasionally, he would fall asleep only to jerk awake with a cry and grip Ruby's arm. She lifted him onto her lap and sang to him after the second time that happened. A soft, nonsensical song that proved she had no gift as a singer. Yet, to Elias and to Buddy, her voice wove an almost magical blanket of contentment over them.

Though she'd spoken of shooting a man and explained about the kidnapping, Ruby didn't mention his declaration on the ride back. When she mentioned the scar on the man's cheek, Elias snorted. "Tyson Monroe! He works for Sauer. I wonder if Mr. Sauer knows his daughter-in-law is in Bailey's Meadow?"

Ruby couldn't answer that. Silence hung between them until she said something that had him thinking hard. "Remember me telling you about the Lord putting us in the right spot to do his will." She broke off and waited until she saw his nod. "Well, tonight sure was a dandy example. There you were, exactly where I needed you."

He hadn't put much store in trusting God since he'd been in the war. Seeing what he had, it didn't seem like a loving god could have allowed those battles.

Maybe he'd been thinking about God all wrong. The Lord dealt with the individual and ministered to each person. It was about the intimate, daily living and how He met the needs then. After all, the Lord had answered his mother's prayers for his safety while he served in the Army. She'd told him that, even when he scoffed at her.

It certainly had him thinking. Seems like it was time to start reading the scriptures to see if these thoughts were true. Could be that Ruby might even like them to read the Bible as a family.

As they rolled into town, he felt eyes on him. Inquiring, friendly eyes. Such a change from Mills Bluff. Men came out of homes at the sight of the wagons rolling past. So little happened in Bailey's Meadow, and never that early!

Mr. Bailey reached Onie's wagon and stared dumbly at Mrs. Sauer, bound and gagged. Then he made a suggestion that had Ruby cheering. "I think we'd better hire Mr. Hastings here as our sheriff. Looks like we need one."

The men debated on what to do about the woman. Howie Owens wanted to drive a post into the ground and leave her tied to it. Walter Fisher suggested they stick her in a basement. "She's your problem, King. Put her down in yours until someone comes to claim her," he grumbled.

Mr. Bailey, the unofficial mayor made the decision, however. "Faith and it seems from the story King's tickled our ears with that she be gammy or an eejit. Aren't you, then, feeling a wee bit sorry for the poor missus?" The men looked at each other, confused by Bailey's words but too afraid to question him lest they offend the man. Elias inwardly smiled but said nothing. After a moment, the men nodded and Bailey smiled with approval at that.

"Fine, then. We'll stick her in the church. Pastor's off to Howard's Place, it being their week for preaching. None there for her to bother." Pointing at two men, he urged, "Crack on, then. One at her shoulders and the other her feet. We'll get her carried off now."

During this Buddy had jerked awake. When the men picked up Mrs. Sauer, he started to cry. "Is the bad woman dead?"

Ruby rubbed his back and made a shushing sound. "No, darling. She's tied up so she can't get to you again. Mama has you and you're safe."

Buddy craned his head to look up at her. "That's what she said. 'Mama's got you.'" He looked over at his father as Elias climbed back into the wagon. In a tiny voice, the boy asked, "Is the bad woman really my mother?"

Taking his son from Ruby, Elias hugged the boy. "You remember your first mother, Buddy my boy. Now, you have Ruby as your new mama. Those women are your real mothers."

A huge sigh of relief erupted from the small chest. The tension of the night flew out of Buddy with that sigh. His usual smile blossomed on his face as he looked at Ruby. "I love my new mama, Daddy. You did good gettin' her for us."

Elias smiled over at Ruby. "That was the Lord, son. We can thank God and the Westward Home and Hearts Matrimonial Agency."

EPILOGUE

Elias waved a letter in her direction. "I heard from Marshal Ferguson today. Mrs. Sauer was convicted and sent to prison rather than an asylum. He says he thinks Monroe is in Kansas." Tyson Monroe had disappeared after his confrontation with Ruby. Marshal Ferguson was still searching for him. At least he hadn't returned to threaten Buddy or Elias.

He frowned at Ruby. "Why you pushed for an asylum instead of prison, I don't know. The woman tried to steal our son."

Ruby didn't bother to explain again to him. Franz Sauer had been unfaithful to a woman who craved his love as well as a child of her own. At least, that's how Ruby had imagined it from the woman's ravings. Certainly, she didn't excuse the murders, but she pitied Mrs. Sauer. After all, Ruby had been childless and alone.

Buddy rushed through the room, pulling Letty in the wagon Onie had purchased for them on his last trip to Plattsmouth. The boy neighed like a horse and tried to race past her.

"Buddy, that's enough of that! No more running in the house." Both children looked at her with disappointed pouts. Nine-month-old Letty lifted her hands to her brother. He put her on the floor and she crawled over to Ruby.

"Mama!" The baby paired her call with uplifted arms. Ruby hoisted her up, settling the girl on her swollen belly. Buddy clung to Ruby's legs and Letty rested on her stomach. The baby inside kicked softly against the pressure of Letty resting against him or her. Childless no more! Ruby gloried in it.

"There was another letter. I'll lay it on the table. From the Sauers." He moved toward her, merely to lay the letter near where she sat. Her husband did drop it there. Instead of leaving quickly, he leaned down and kissed her, a touch of mouths that reaffirmed his love and devotion. Then he left, returning to the forge he'd had built two months ago.

This letter from the Sauers must not have been as disturbing as their previous ones. Elias' voice didn't betray hurt or anger. Past letters, which arrived weekly, had been accusatory or had contained pleas to send them Buddy.

The couple had stormed into Bailey's Meadow a day after their daughter-in-law kidnapped Buddy. With Tyson Monroe and two thugs accompanying them, Mr. Sauer appeared in the door of the livery, telling his stooges to grab Elias. At Ruby's urgent screams, Onie rounded up the men of their town and moved to stop the lynching.

Thank goodness Marshal Ferguson had arrived on the same train in Plattsmouth. He rode up in time to add his authority to Onie's actions. Once Elias explained about the young Mrs. Sauer and the marshal told of the evidence he'd collected, Sauer grudgingly admitted that it didn't seem hanging was in order after all. No apology was given, of course.

After nearly hanging Elias, Sauer had the nerve to announce he and his wife planned to move to

Bailey's Meadow. Unless, he offered, Elias gave them Buddy. Mr. Bailey and Sheriff Onie Hastings coldly let them know they wouldn't be welcomed in town. Onie refused to tell his sister what had been said or if he'd used threats to change Sauer's plans. She had to be satisfied that the couple and their stooges left without caring what happened to their daughter-in-law.

At a knock on the back door, Ruby moved through the kitchen. Buddy giggled as he hung on like a burr and forced her to drag him along with her. Opening it, she welcomed Mother Schmidt. "Come in. What has you out in the snow?"

Buddy left his mother's leg and hugged his grandmother. She beamed but still gently chastised him. "Now, let me get my coat off. How is Grandma supposed to hug you with my coat and mittens still on?"

As she removed her outer garments, the woman held out a small, red garment. "I finished the sweater for Letty this afternoon and wanted to bring it over." Handing over the sweater, Mrs. Schmidt caressed Letty's cheek and then leaned down to hug her grandson.

Removing the sweater Mrs. Schmidt had made last week, Ruby dressed Letty in the new one. It hung a bit looser on the child and would be more comfortable, Ruby thought. "Thank you. You are so kind to us."

The woman waved the words away and sat at the table to enjoy a cup of coffee and a chat. She did this often, and Ruby valued her companionship.

Four months before, when the Schmidts first arrived in Bailey's Meadow, an awkward tension existed between the women. For whatever reason, Elias hadn't written to tell them he'd married. They'd freighted their household goods, intending to live with him and keep house for the two Kline men. Thank goodness Howie Owens had seized on their arrival to sell them his place. They'd only needed to live together for a week before the older couple settled into their own home.

And they took the red velvet sofa that reminded Ruby of fussy Mrs. Cummings. Her subdued blue sofa replaced it, along with pictures she'd uncrated and hung on the walls. It had become her parlor, comforting and peaceful.

After their move, Ruby extended many invitations to the couple. She wanted them to be a part of Buddy's life. To do that, she walked the boy over to his grandparents' home almost daily, until winter set in with a fierceness that frightened her. As the land froze, her relationship with Mother Schmidt thawed and grew almost loving. The woman adored both children and appreciated Ruby's willingness to share them, or so she said. Her attitude relieved and delighted Ruby.

"What a bunch of storms we've had! With this spot of clear weather, Grandpa arrived back from Plattsmouth a bit ago. Good thing. My bones tell me another squall's brewing." Mother Schmidt poured a cup of coffee and added her usual teaspoon of sugar from the bowl in the center of the table. "He does enjoy being the town's freighter. Thinks he's some sort of government agent because he brings the mail."

Onie had been only too happy to hand the job over to Father Schmidt. Ruby smiled as she remembered the relief on the older man's face at having a job to do, even if he didn't need the money after selling his properties in Mills Bluff.

Easing into a seat at the table, her baby kicked against the edge of the table that pushed on her stomach. This baby liked to have his or her space. What a temper!

As Ruby rubbed at her belly, the older woman smiled. "Kicking and fussing again today? What a little pepper pot that one is." She laughed and squeezed her grandson who sat on her lap. "I like 'em busy and feisty, like our Buddy here."

"Grandma, I don't wanna be Buddy anymore." At the boy's serious tone and strange words, the women frowned at him.

"What do you mean? Who do you want to be?" Mrs. Schmidt prodded.

"I wanna be Frank again. Like you used to call me." The boy put a hand on either side of his grandmother's face and stared at her intently. "Remember? Back when we lived somewhere else and didn't have Mama and Letty."

Mother Schmidt nodded. The boy's request concerned Ruby. She worked to keep worry out of her voice as she good-naturedly said, "But you've always been my Buddy. I don't know Frank."

He looked at his mama, confused. "You know me! I'll still me, but I'm five now, Mama. I'm a big boy and don't want a baby name."

Relief flooded her. Fear that he wanted a life without her like he'd had in Mills Bluff had gripped Ruby. Even with their loving relationship, a part of Ruby feared something creating a wedge between them. She'd have to think about that. Maybe Elias could help her understand her fear.

Elias. Oh, what a husband! She'd come west to find a home and had found her heart. God bless the day she'd stood over her parents' graves and met a woman with a vision of settling the west. She'd taken a risk on that woman.

The warmth of her kitchen surrounded her with contentment. Smiling at her son and at Grandma, as the woman insisted everyone call her, Ruby soaked in the joy of it. She patted Letty's back and gloried in the kick from her newest child.

Thank God for Mrs. Crenshaw. Listening to the older woman had given Ruby the impossible—a husband and children. Her risk on a man in the West brought her the joy of loving and knowing she was loved in return. Quite a change for a spinster with no future. Life certainly was good in the West.

LEAVE A REVIEW

The End

If you enjoyed this story, I would appreciate it if you would leave a review, as it helps me reach new readers and continue to write stories that appeal to you.

Tap here to leave a review.

https://www.amazon.com/Marisa-Masterson/e/B07PRCNS49

Grace for a Drifter
The Belles of Wyoming #15

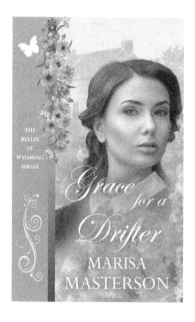

Turn the page for the first chapter of Marisa's
Book in The Belles of Wyoming Summer Series!

CHAPTER 1

"Watch your step, ma'am!" A hand came out to steady Grace Winkleman as she made her way down the steps of the only hotel in Fort Bridger.

Smiling, she thanked the doorman. Intent on saying goodbye to her friend and fellow teacher, Amelia Grayson, the steps took Grace by surprise. Slightly lifting her cotton, navy skirt, she made her way down the remaining steps. At the bottom, she waved to her worried-looking friend to let her know she was fine. Amelia waved back and entered the hotel's door.

It had been a fine week. One of the things she enjoyed about teaching in Wyoming was the yearly get together required of educators. The small teacher convention allowed for the discussion of lesson plans and activities as well as for learning new theories and methods. Though it might not be a state yet, Wyoming certainly was a progressive territory.

Grasping her carpetbag in her left hand, Grace raised her right to fan her face. The August heat seemed unusually brutal for the late morning. Crossing the street, she made her way to the dry goods store about a block from the hotel. Paps Johnson told her to meet him there if she wanted a ride back to Belle.

Belle! The musical sound of the town's name brought a sweet smile to her face. It became a haven for her three years ago when she needed a new start after the incident. Silly spinster that she'd been, she'd fallen hard for the fast talker. The town had advertised for a teacher at the very time that she had needed to start over far from her home state of Missouri.

Even though the small town provided her with only a handful of pupils, she had a house to live in and a decent wage. The commitment by townsfolk to those few children and their education impressed her three years ago and continued to touch her deeply. The people of Belle made the town a truly wonderful place to live.

Seeing Paps at his wagon, she lifted a hand in greeting. The old man nodded in her direction and came around his wagon to help her out of the street and onto the boardwalk. Without a word, he took the carpetbag from her grasp and set it gently into his wagon, amongst the other goods he would transport back to Belle.

"Timing's good, Miss Winkleman. I just now finished loading and was thinking as how I'd like to be on the road home." He flashed a semi-toothless grin at her as he spoke.

"I am gratified not to keep you waiting, Mr. Johnson, and I do appreciate the ride. It has been a wonderful week here in Fort Bridger, but I am ready to head home." As she spoke, Grace allowed Paps to help her up into the wagon. She settled herself on the hard seat and spread her skirts about her.

Turning away from her, Paps bellowed a deeply spoken farewell to the store owner before looking back at the schoolteacher. "Sure you don't need to buy anything at this here store afore I start the team a moving?"

She shook her head. "No, I had a chance yesterday to shop. The conference lasted only five days, so I had one free to explore Fort Bridger with Miss Grayson. Perhaps you've met her, the teacher in Glenda?"

Paps grunted and moved his head to indicate he hadn't. Without another word, he clicked to his team of mules and tapped the leathers softly to their backs. Her week of vacation might be over, yet Grace didn't care. She'd be glad to be home in Belle.

If she had looked over her shoulder at that moment, she might have been concerned. As it was, she stared straight ahead and spoke to Paps of the exciting ideas she'd learned that week. The old man might not be an educator, true. Still, he listened and nodded his head in the correct spots of the conversation.

Behind her, the store proprietor and a black-haired man stood on the boardwalk and watched the wagon leave. The man pointed in her direction and spoke with a trembling voice. Shock marked his expression. The store owner answered his questions, supplying the schoolteacher's name and the town where she lived. He smiled over the idea that someone would be interested in a spinster teacher.

He didn't understand that the other man had just seen a ghost.

On the thirty-mile trip to Belle, Grace asked about the happenings in the town over the last week. Paps rubbed his jaw and thought. "Suppose the buzz round town is mostly Martin's accident. Too, everyone's excited for the cake walk and dance this weekend. Folks enjoy winning things, even if it's only someone's lopsided cake."

Paps shifted on the seat and angled his head to spit over the side of the wagon. Grace looked away and pretended not to see the man rid his mouth of the clump of tobacco. Once his mouth was free, he continued with the news from Belle.

"Heard tell that Hoyt Cole plans to get married. Other than that, the only happening I can recall was the latest story of Spencer Brannon. Can't believe that boy thinks he can work a herd. Falls from his horse more than he rides the range." Then the man began to retell the story of Spencer's latest debacle.

Grace shook her head in response to Paps' story. She felt sorry for the man who tried hard to live up to his cousins. She was glad for the fundraiser. The cake walk would be the perfect time to visit with parents and pupils alike. She liked to connect with each family before the start of a new term and appreciated not needing to rent a buggy to do that.

The freighter finished his tale and looked at her, surprised when she didn't laugh. She smiled weakly at him, realizing she'd been lost in her thoughts and hadn't listened. Apologizing, she encouraged him to tell her more about news from the outlying ranches around Belle. He grunted deep in his throat but started another story. Grace moved the warm air around her face with her beautifully painted fan and forced her mind to concentrate. She knew the man loved an audience for his stories and would continue to talk until they reached Belle. Concentrating became forced as she looked at the fan and remembered the man who gave it to her on the night that changed her life.

By the deep guffaws coming from Paps, she realized she'd missed his story. What a terrible companion for the man! She'd turned maudlin today, remembering that terrible time in her life. Perhaps she should get rid of the fan to forget about the man who presented it to her. A jolt of grief knifed through her at the thought of parting with this last connection to him.

Belle Creek lay just ahead of them. Beyond that, she saw the outline of buildings and knew they were almost home. Grace swallowed a sigh of relief, not wanting the kind livery owner to hear it. Paps had been kind to bring her from Fort Bridger. Still, fatigue and sentiment made her long to be alone.

Like a gentleman, he directed the mules to the schoolhouse and her small dwelling that connected to the back of it. The coziness of those two rooms drew her and she quickly thanked her driver and hurried into the rear of the school.

The one long room had been divided for the teacher. She entered into her combination kitchen and sitting room. To the far end stood a wall with a door placed into it. On the other side was her bedroom. It shared a wall with the large schoolroom. Truly, it was all the space she needed to be comfortable and allowed her privacy she wouldn't have if she'd needed to board with various families as some teachers did.

That had been the way she'd lived in Missouri. At first, the school board had required her to move each month to stay with a different family. Since her aunt lived within the district, Grace had been able to convince them that she should simply live with her. By then Errol had started romancing her and she hoped to hide her romantic activities by not living with the nosy families. Months after Errol disappeared it became impossible to hide the result from anyone in the town.

Thinking about that result brought her aunt's last letter to mind. She'd been full of complaints. The farm didn't bring in enough income. She didn't have a washing machine like her neighbor, Edna Martin, did. Uncle Ralph had grown miserly and spiteful. The list of grievances continued.

The woman's complaints didn't surprise her. What Grace longed for in the letters was a mention of Robby. Her aunt had wanted a baby for so long. Now that she had her son, why didn't Aunt Milly mention him? The three-year-old must be accomplishing new things all the time and Grace was greedy for any hint about his life.

Tears flowed down her face. Enough of this! Grace stiffened her spine and unpacked her carpetbag. Having the hotel launder her clothes before she returned to Belle had been a splurge. As she put away clean garments, she reveled in the luxury of not needing to hunch over her scrub board for another week. Tomorrow she could focus on arranging the schoolroom.

The next morning, Grace carried a basket of staples over one arm and strolled to the school. She'd had a visit with Livvy and learned more about the dance that Saturday. From the sounds of it, she should be able to meet with every family from the area that night. Before the evening was over, she would have a reliable grasp of who to expect for school in September.

Looking toward the livery, Grace noticed a wagon parked there. That in itself wasn't surprising.

The letter on the canvas held her attention. It was a traveling cobbler. Had she ever heard of a cobbler who went from town to town?

Nearing the school, she watched a young girl soar on the swing hung from a tree beside the building. Giggles floated on the air as she pumped skinny legs to send her higher. The merry sound ceased as the girl saw Grace approach.

Once her feet were back on the dirt below the swing, the little one stood with her head bowed. "Sorry, ma'am, for helping myself to your swing."

Grace put out her free hand and, with a finger, tipped up the girl's face. "That swing is for anyone who wants to use it. This is the school after all, so it belongs to everyone in town."

A smile brightened the sweet face and the girl plopped back onto the board seat of the swing. Grace watched her pump her short legs and decided to question her. "What is your name? I'm afraid I don't remember meeting your family."

As black curls blew back from her face, the girl giggled. "We came to town today. I'm Liza."

"Are your parents shopping at the mercantile?" Families from outlying farms and ranches came in for supplies and often sent their children over to play in the schoolyard while they shopped.

"Daddy's working. Shoes, shoes, shoes!" Liza sang those three words as she shot up into the air.

At least that answered who she belonged to and when she'd arrived. Obviously, the traveling cobbler must be her father.

"Are there other children in your family, Liza?" Perhaps the cobbler had decided to move here and start a shop. She welcomed the idea of more students.

Evidently, Liza had grown tired of flying into the air. Now she used her legs to twist the rope of the swing. Lifting her feet, she shrieked with laughter as the rope unwound and she flew in circles. When the girl once again sat looking at Grace, she asked her question again.

Liza shrugged. "Don't think so. Just Daddy and me."

"And your mother?" Grace didn't know why she felt driven to find out if the man was married. At that moment, the information seemed vital.

"Nah. Mommy died. Daddy's wife died too. He says, 'I'm cursed'." The girl said the last words in a deep, sad voice, obviously imitating her father.

Grace laid a comforting hand on the child's back. "Yes, when a mommy dies, the daddy does lose his wife." At her words, Liza shook her head and frowned.

She'd upset the child and Grace suddenly felt ashamed. "We won't speak of that anymore. Do you think you'll be coming to my school next month?"

"We'll be on our way." Liza became chanting, "On our way, never stay," saying the phrase over and over. When she stopped, she shrugged. "I never go to school."

Feeling sad for the girl, Grace offered what she could. "Come to see me every day and we can play school. I'll teach you while you're in town."

At the word "play" Liza's face brightened. She nodded her head, causing her black curls to bounce.

Unable to resist, Grace laid a tender hand to those curls. She remembered another head full of black wavy hair as it bent over her to kiss her waiting lips.

With a gasp, she realized where her wild thoughts had wandered. Liza heard the gasp and looked at her oddly. Needing an explanation, she quickly searched her mind. "You have such beautiful hair. Would you like me to wash it for you? Then I can put it into braids and ribbons."

The boisterous girl looked in the direction of the cobbler's wagon and then nodded shyly. Grace held out her hand. When Liza placed her smaller one in Grace's she led her into her home and prepared for a day spent with her new young friend. Gracious but she'd been maudlin lately. Caring for Liza and tutoring her would be exactly the tonic she needed to forget.

ABOUT MARISA

Marisa Masterson and her husband of thirty years reside in Saginaw, Michigan. They have two grown children, one son-in-law, a grandchild on the way, and one old and lazy dog.

She is a retired high school English teacher and oversaw a high school writing center in partnership with the local university. In addition, she is a National Writing Project fellow.

Focusing on her home state of Wisconsin, she writes sweet historical romance. Growing up, she loved hearing stories about her family pioneering in that state. Those stories, in part, are what inspired her to begin writing.

Find her on Facebook, in the Chat Sip and Read Community, Sweet Wild West Reads, or on her Facebook page.

If you like this book, please take a few minutes to leave a review now! Marisa appreciates it and you may help a reader find their next favorite book!

Ruby's Risk

This book is a work of fiction. The names, characters, places, and incidents are all products of the author's imagination and are not to be construed as real. Any resemblances to persons, organizations, events, or locales are entirely coincidental.

The book contains material protected under International and Federal Copyright Laws and Treaties. All rights are reserved with the exceptions of quotes used in reviews. No part of this book may be reproduced or transmitted in any form or by any means, electronic or mechanical, including photocopying, recording, or by any information storage system without express written permission from the author.

Ruby's Risk ©2019 Marisa Masterson
Cover Design by Virginia McKevitt
        http://www.virginiamckevitt.com
Editing by Amy Petrowich
Formatting by Christine Sterling

1st Ed.

Made in United States
Orlando, FL
01 February 2024

43143043R00139